B

NEIL JAMES

This book is a work of fiction. Names, characters, businesses, places, events, locales, and incidents are either the products of the author's imagination or used in a fictitious manner. Any resemblance to actual persons, living or dead, or actual events is purely coincidental.
ISBN-9798517637604

Carry the battle to them. Don't let them bring it to you.
Put them on the defensive, and don't ever apologize for anything.

Harry S. Truman

BRACKETT

Prologue

In May of the year 1863, 29 men ventured from the gold fields of the Boise Basin to the Owyhee Mountains of Southwestern Idaho Territory. They were led by a man named Michael Jordan and searched for the fabled Blue Bucket load.

Legend had it that a lost group of covered wagons stumbled into a creek bed where gold nuggets were so abundant, they were used as sinkers for their fishing lines. Although a small number of the group eventually made it to their Oregon destination with a bit of gold. They had traveled around and through so many mountains and deserts, trying to find their way that none could remember from where it came. They did recall hanging a blue bucket on a tree near the campsite. Hence, the name still stimulates the imagination of treasure hunters to this day. If the area ever actually existed, its location remains a secret of the western mountains.

The Michael Jordan men never found the Blue Bucket, but they did find their own bonanza creek with enough gold at its bottom to make them forget about searching for the Blue Bucket. They became known as the Discovery Group, a title that still endures a century and a half later.

These men posted their claims, set up rules, and when they returned to the Boise Basin for supplies, word of their find spread like wildfire. Within two weeks, over two thousand miners arrived. These newcomers worked their way up the creek another six miles and set up a trading center they called Ruby City. The village offered a small space to expand, and the following year a new town, half a mile farther up the creek, started growing in competition. It was, and is, called Silver City.

From those first days and weeks, the men and later families were constantly harassed by the local Indians. Paiutes, Shoshonis, and Bannacks (In centuries past, the spelling most used was Bannack. Over the decades, the modern spelling has become Bannock.) For thousands of years, the mountains had sustained the native peoples, and they were still trying to hold on to their lives and livelihood. Most just wanted to preserve the way of life known to their forefathers. They rightly felt that the White Man would drive them away if they didn't fight for their land. Away to where they had no idea. So, they fought. They fought a battle they slowly came to realize could never be won.

As they referred to themselves, the People mainly lived quiet lives, going about their daily chores in the same frame of mind as their White counterparts. Each person had their duties, and most contributed to the entire community's well-being. Hunting parties shared all they took, as did the women harvesting balsam and camas roots, mountain berries, and a plethora of edible plants.

Not all followed the long-existing system, though, like the world of the White Man, some lived lives outside the accepted morals of Indian life. One such was feared more than all the rest. He went by numerous names, but the White men called him Bigfoot because of his colossal size. The Indians, depending on their dialect, called him Owlux or Nampuh. He led a band of renegades leaving death and destruction in his wake.

Because of his mass, nearly seven feet tall and over three hundred pounds of solid muscle, his chosen mode of transport was walking or running, as the horses of the day could not realistically carry him far. It was believed he could outlast any pony over a long distance.

In the years leading up to 1868, newspapers blamed him for numerous atrocities throughout the Southwestern Idaho Territory and what is now Southeastern Oregon. The mounted Army chased him and successfully dismantled his bands more than once but could never apprehend the giant himself.

Always, following these Army raids, he gathered more human riff-raff and continued attacks on wagon trains, outposts, and weary travelers. No longer did he lead only Indians. True, his conglomeration did consist of Indians, but in addition, a third of his current band were a hodgepodge of Mexicans, Whites, Blacks, and mixtures of all. These non-Indians, just a mass of outcasts, had no allegiance to the cause of tribal Indians. They robbed and murdered for their own greed and satisfaction. They seemed to kill with pleasure, and only for potential profit did they let a victim live.

Now, the young Sheriff of Silver City, Idaho was on the trail of this outlaw group and their notorious leader. A pursuit that would most certainly end in death. But whose death would it be?

CHAPTER ONE

The sweat made him shiver, burned his eyes, and soaked the bedding. He looked at the ceiling for a long time before willing himself to sit up.

He thought about the pure hatred that brought him to Silver City. He no longer took pleasure in killing, but he had then. The day he walked into the Idaho Hotel's saloon and shot Lacy Bernhardt. He enjoyed that. The man who had killed his family. The man who had clubbed and then shot his mother.

Clay Brackett stood by helplessly in his dream and watched the man with the red beard kill his mother. He then watched his adopted father be tied, arms and legs, between four horses and ripped apart. His mother and his father had died, but the dream would not.

Why all these years later had he started having this recurring nightmare? Had he not hunted down and taken his revenge on the men responsible for killing his family? Did not this very room exist directly above the saloon where it happened?

Always, he had been able to handle his emotions, but not when it came to this. Not when it came to the dream. Only when drowning in his favorite bourbon, did he get a reprieve. The dream wouldn't leave him alone, whether sleeping or making his rounds of the town as sheriff. Nagging at him until he could wash it away with whiskey.

He swung his legs to the side of the mattress, wiped his eyes, and steadied himself for a few seconds, hoping his head would stop swimming. He felt pleased to see he had at least taken off his boots, gun belt, shirt, and pants before passing out on the bed. He searched the floor, past his boots and pile of clothes. He turned his head slowly and looked on the bed beside his pillow.

He leaned to the pillow with a grunt and picked up the nearly empty bourbon bottle. No cork. He held it up to the window light. Still a hint of liquid. The teaspoon's worth of bourbon swallowed and down the wrong way brought on a coughing spasm, making him grab his forehead. The pain in his stomach hit him like a nine-pound hammer with each cough doubling him over.

As the coughing subsided, he slowly caught his breath, stood to a bent position, and carefully made his way to the empty basin, but the pitcher still had some water in it. He washed his face, raised his head enough to look in the mirror, saw a drawn face, full beard, and yellowed eyes.

He had, at one time, shaved his dark brown beard and mustache but recently found it just too much of an effort. Both at full growth made him look older than his twenty-five years.

"Why did I spend all that money on you, mirror? Just to have you mock me with this false reflection. You are a fabricator of untruths!"

He hadn't spoken loudly, but enough to remind him his head had not yet mended from the coughing. He again steadied himself with both hands on the sides of the basin stand. Then, with determination, the Sheriff of Silver City, Idaho, straightened his tall frame, turned, took a deep breath, and began the ordeal of getting dressed.

While he slowly worked his way into his boots, his thoughts turned to the only vital thing in his miserable life. Beth. The only woman he thought he could ever love. Now, he felt her slipping away, day by day. His emotions were not understandable to her. His fits of anger, his times when he refused to talk with her. Hell, he couldn't understand his feelings either. His drinking had to stop, but how could he face the dreams without it?

He turned once more to the mirror, leaned close in to examine the face.

"Just who the hell are you. You are not Indian, and you are not a white man. It is time to figure out what you want."

He left his room and unsteadily made his way down to the adjoining saloon.

A voice offered, "Well, you look like a pile of cow dung."

Brackett raised his eyes and looked at the full-time bar manager, who doubled as his part-time deputy. Behind the Idaho Hotel's saloon bar stood his only true friend in the entire city.

"Thanks for the assessment. How about some of that rotgut poison you call coffee?"

Phil Bannon slid a cup of the steaming stuff across the bar.

"What time is it?" Brackett fished in his pockets. "I can't find my watch."

"It's nearly noon, and I have your watch. You lost it to me last night. I had two pairs, and you just one."

"Well, I want it back. What do you want for it?"

Phil reached in his shirt pocket and handed the watch across the bar. "I'll put it on your tab."

Brackett gave the watch a quick shake and listened for its tick. Securing it in his vest, he took a sip of the coffee and winced.

"Anything I need to know about, other than you stealing my watch?"

"Not so far." Phil thought for a second, "Oh, well, that kid that sweeps floors for Mrs. Yonkers came by a little while ago. Says that old Indian that's been hanging around town for the last week or so, the one that claims to be a Modoc chief? Says he stole her cat and then tried to sell it back to her. Says she wants him put away."

Brackett took another sip of the coffee.

"All right, I will go round him up after I have some coffee. Put something in this, will you?"

Phil reached to the back bar and added a shot of bourbon to Brackett's cup. "I know you're just in your twenties, but you keep drinkin' like this, you ain't never gonna see thirty."

Brackett gave him a stiff look, turned his back to him, and leaned against the bar. Sipping his laced coffee, he surveyed what he could of the street traffic. Dust already beginning to rise. "Wind picking up. Drying out the road. Hate the wind. Hate the dust."

Turning back around, he slid his half-empty cup across to Phil, "One more time, with both."

Phil had no idea how right was his observation about his friend's drinking. Just six days before, continually suffering from gut-wrenching stomach pain, the young sheriff, while playing faro in the saloon, had brought up the subject to Doc Simpson. The doctor laid down his cards and looked closely at Brackett's eyes.

"You lost any weight of late?"

"Some, not much. Haven't felt like eating lately."

"You best stop in my office so as I can take a better look at ya."

Four days had elapsed when he again ran into the doctor. "Haven't noticed ya in my office. When ya coming in?"

Brackett tipped his hat. "Afternoon, Doc. Been pretty busy. How about next week?"

Doc shook his head. "How about right now? My office is right here. Won't take long for a quick look."

The examination took less than twenty minutes, the prognosis included.

"Clay, I'm afraid what I'm seeing here is not good."

Brackett said nothing but continued buttoning his shirt.

Doc continued, "Look, your eyes are yellow. Jaundiced. You're having severe stomach pains and have been for quite some time. You're losing weight, and your appetite is diminished. I can feel some swelling under your ribs right here on the right side."

"So, what do you think it is? I do not think it is bad food. I eat all my meals at Beth's place."

Doc took off his glasses. "I wish it was. I could treat that. No son, I believe that you are suffering from liver problems. I could be wrong. A bum gall bladder can produce similar symptoms, and so can other things. I can't tell you the cause for certain. But I can tell you this, your hard-drinking, I'm certain, has contributed heavily."

Brackett glanced at the wall where a glass-encased certificate resided without reading it.

"All right, so what is the cure? I understand. You're telling me that I need to cut down on my drinking?"

"Cut down?" His voice rose considerably, and deep furrows appeared on the older man's forehead. "Tarnation Boy! I'm telling you to stop drinking altogether! Right away! Today! This very minute! Who knows, maybe that might help. You're young and tough, and you just might recover. The liver can heal itself up until the time it cannot. Understand this, every drink you take will put you closer to going over the edge with no way to climb back up. And Clay, that's true no matter what is going on inside your body. Furthermore, if you don't mind me saying, that includes your well-being outside your body."

Brackett suspected a hint about his relationship with Beth but let it pass.

"What else can I do? Or, what else can you do for me?"

Doc looked at the ceiling as if searching for guidance and tugged his grey beard in frustration.

"Clay, fact is, I've never seen a case such as this in somebody your age. The ones I've seen have been folks at least in their forties. If it is what I think it might be, and if it is as developed as I believe it could be, I can't do a damn thing for you. It's going to be up to you."

Brackett swatted away a pestering fly. "Well, if it is what you think it is, what should I expect?"

Doc set his glasses on his desk. "You'll continue to suffer from the same symptoms as now, but they will get worse. Probably within a few weeks. Months at best."

"Will I die from it?"

Doc glanced at the floor and then back up to meet Brackett's eyes. "If you don't change the way you're living or get yourself killed by some idiot's bullet first, and, if I'm reading what I see properly, then yes, I believe you will die from it. I'm surely sorry, son."

Brackett nodded his understanding. "How will it happen?"

"No need to go into that. You'll know it as it progresses if it does. All I can tell you is to stop that damn drinking right now, and you might have a chance. Otherwise, might want to get your affairs in order. Let somebody know how to notify your people if you have any."

Brackett walked over to the window and watched Red Hand Jack tap a stick on the head of his big black ox as the beast lumbered along, kicking up puffs of dust with every hoof fall. Three more oxen, attached to the same heavy freight wagon, strained along with the leader.

Brackett continued looking at the procession. "You ever noticed how close Red Hand Jack gets to that big ox of his. A wonder he has not been in here to have you fix a stepped-on foot."

"Did you hear what I said?" replied Doc.

Brackett turned back to face the man. "Yes, sir, I heard, and I will do that, but I still want to know what to expect if worse comes to worst."

"All right. Well, you might start noticing some confusion, maybe difficulty in figuring things. Fuzzy headiness. That kind of thing. Could be severe at times, but mostly you'll be clear-headed. It'll come and go. You may have temper flairs about things that never bothered you before. Your ankles and feet may swell, even while you continue to lose weight. Nausea, more intense stomach pain, sweating, fever, chills... in the end, you could even lose consciousness and fall into a coma. I've seen all of those things. Not ever all in one person, you understand. And never in someone as young as you. It's different for everybody. If the stomach pain gets too much, come on in, and I can give you a bottle of laudanum. It'll help for a while."

Brackett nodded, "All right, thanks, Doc. I will let you know if I need the pain killer."

As he reached for the doorknob, Doc gave his parting shot, “You quit drinking, this might all go away.”

Brackett had spent his life beating the odds and decided this would be no different. He would quit drinking, and everything would be fine. So far, he hadn’t gotten around to testing the theory. Maybe next week, he might give sobriety a try. That he had become addicted to alcohol, he had no doubts but believed he could and would beat the thing. If only the nightmares would leave him to get some rest. If only that would bring Beth back to him.

On the other hand, death had never been something he dreaded. Every living thing on earth would eventually meet its end. Some sooner than others. He had himself been responsible for a few meeting their early demise. He had always been determined to make sure his years in this realm be of his choosing. Fear had never yet been a part of his consciousness. At least, not fear for himself.

But of late, the part about living every day as best he could had somehow escaped him. For months, he had just been following the same routine, going through the motions without emotion. He no longer wanted to be a sheriff. Truth be told, he had never wanted to be a sheriff. He no longer wanted to live in this mining town. In fact, he no longer wanted to live in any town. Now, with the stomach pains and headaches and hangovers he never used to experience, he just wanted to be away. Into the mountains of his youth to live that simple life again. He pictured a couple of kids playing next to a creek while he and Beth sat watching from the porch of their cabin. He kicked an empty bean can off the boardwalk in anger. He wondered at his naivety. If he kept to his way of living, he would be lucky if Beth would even allow him in her café.

Brackett had already noticed how it took him longer, each hungover morning, to get his wits about him. He hadn't offered that bit of information to Doc Simpson. He also knew he tended to have some unexplained mood changes.

Two nights earlier, he knocked a drunken kid to the floor with his revolver. Seeing the boy staggering from the bar, Brackett told him to head home.

"Sure, Sheriff, I'll jist say my nighty nights to muh friends first."

The kid, maybe seventeen or eighteen, turned to walk back to his friends. Brackett had suddenly erupted in anger, grabbed the kid by the shoulder, spun him around, and dropped his gun barrel on the side of his head. The kid went down like he'd been shot.

He helped the boy to his wobbly feet and walked him to the kid's tent. He didn't feel particularly bad about banging the youngster on the head. He used that technique with many a drunk over the years. Had the kid not been ready to fall over anyway, the blow would have only gotten his attention. No, but why had he done it? The boy had not been belligerent or unruly. Somehow, Brackett had to straighten out his life. And it needed to be done soon, or face losing Beth forever.

CHAPTER TWO

Beth found nothing surprising when Brackett didn't show up for breakfast or the midday dinner. His drinking had intensified considerably in the past year. Only she knew about the nightmares. She also suspected his hangovers were worsening, and the thought of eating before mid-day most likely made his stomach churn.

His sudden mood swings and lack of patience were hurting her immensely. Beth felt certain these personality changes resulted from the drinking, and the drinking resulted from the nightmares. She had begged him to at least cut back. He told her he would be working on it, but she had yet to see any sign of that happening. Still, she couldn't give up on him. She loved him.

Beth had seen so many signs of his goodness. He looked out for the people others shunned. She had found out about one of his acts of benevolence strictly by accident when a messenger delivered a note meant for Clay. It came to the café instead of his hotel room.

In a hurry and not realizing it wasn't meant for her, Beth read it, sorely confused until she looked at the top and found it addressed to Clay. A receipt for his recent deposit to the Stone Family account. Embarrassed she had accidentally read his private material, she never told him what she had found.

The Stone family, the mother, and five young children had the money for food, shelter, and clothes because Clay provided it out of his own pocket. Mrs. Stone had no idea from whom the funds came.

Shortly after her husband died in the mine cave-in, Mrs. Stone received notification the house they had been renting now belonged to them. More overwhelming, the notice went on to say money had been deposited in the bank in her name. When she went to see how any of this could be true, the banker handed over a note.

"Dear Mrs. Stone,

I knew your husband to be a good and generous man. I offer my sympathy. Please accept the money in your new bank account as my way of sending condolences. Your home is now yours. The taxes on it have been paid ahead. When you are able to recover from your loss, let the bank know, and I will stop putting money in your account. There is no hurry. Until then, please continue to raise your children as best you can. All my best to you all."

Signed, *"A friend of good people"*

That would be the Clay Brackett she came to love. The Clay Brackett she knew she would love forever. But, he changed, slowly at first and now more rapidly. Still generous to a fault but different in so many other ways. She just didn't know if she could live with the man she saw developing.

The one bright spot in Beth's life, the arrival of her younger brother, Drew, from Oregon. He worked on a fishing boat at the coast but injured his right leg. He recovered enough to walk, albeit with a stiff knee, but not the agility needed to work on the ever-rocking fishing boat. When Beth received the letter about the accident, she wrote back and urged him to come help her run the café. It took another two letters to convince him, but he finally arrived. The regular customers took to him almost immediately. They constantly wanted more of his sea stories, and Drew Alexander became a master storyteller, even at the tender age of nineteen.

Clay Brackett went to the valley to escort the young man to Silver City, and became friends by the time they concluded the trip. While the talkative Drew entertained Brackett with his tales, his new friend offered nothing about his past.

One night, while helping his sister with the dishes, he asked, "What's his story? I mean, what's his background. He sure seems young to be the sheriff of such a town like this."

"Well," she began, "He is young, but he was even younger when they talked him into being sheriff. Just twenty-one, as a matter of fact."

"Twenty-one? What did they see in him?"

"Well, let me tell you a little about his bringing up. His father was killed in a raid on their wagon train when he was just a baby. Somehow, his mother got away, and a brave from another tribe ran across her and baby Clay and took them to his summer camp. Actually, it was only a few miles as the crow flies from Silver City. Of course, Silver City didn't exist then. The only white people were on wagon trains down on the Snake. Anyway, as I understand it, Clay's mother eventually ended up marrying the Indian that found them, and by then, the brave had become a mighty chief of their tribe."

"Well, how did he end up in Silver City?"

She chuckled, handed him another plate to dry, and said, "Just hang on, I'll get there."

Drew grinned, took the plate, and nodded.

"So, as I was saying, his mother married the chief and had two or three more children by him. He adopted Clay as his own, and they were pretty much inseparable. Clay learned all the ways of the Indian life until he was about sixteen."

"Sixteen? What happened then?"

Beth put a finger to her lips. He smiled and nodded again.

"Sixteen. That's when the wagon master, from the time his white father was killed, showed up with his own son to find Clay and his mother. He'd been looking off and on for them all that time."

He stacked the last plate on the clean ones, and she took off her apron. Opening the icebox, she retrieved two bottles of sarsaparilla they had made the day before. She led him into the closed dining room of the café, and they sat at a table facing each other.

Drew took a gulp of the drink. “Then what happened?”

“Well, the grownups agreed that Clay would go with the wagon master and his son and go to the white man’s school. Of course, Clay wanted no part of that to begin with, but with his mother and adopted father urging him on, he finally consented and went with them.”

“Seems strange that the Indian would want to let him go with the white people. Never heard of anything like that before.”

“Buha, that was the chief’s Indian name felt like it would be good to have his white son wise in the ways of white people. He knew the time would come when his tribe would be forced to negotiate with them.”

“I guess that makes sense. Where did they take him?”

“They took him to Santa Fe, where they lived. The wagon master had become a marshal there. Clay’s mother had given him a good education when it came to reading and writing and numbers and such, so he did surprisingly well and finished high school with the wagon master’s son. Then the two of them went to college for four years. Both the other boy and Clay got degrees in law. While at college, they passed their time by practicing the art of quick draw. Even had special holsters built just for that purpose. Nobody had ever seen anything like that, and they made money putting on exhibitions for folks there. At least enough money to pay for the ammunition they used."

"Well, how on earth does a lawyer from Santa Fe end up in Silver City?"

"Patience, my dear, patience. He never forgot his Indian family here in these mountains and couldn't wait to return to them. But just a week before he arrived, his whole family was murdered by some no goods. Murdered in the most brutal of ways. I won't go into that part. Anyway, he found out who the men were and found out gold had been discovered in his mountains, and Silver City had sprung up while he was away. He heard that the men who killed his family were here, so he came here for vengeance. He found them, and there was a terrible shootout right over there in the saloon at the Idaho Hotel. When he walked out, the men that killed his family were dead."

Drew sat back in his chair and studied his sister. "So, he kills a bunch of guys, and they make him sheriff for it?"

"Well, kind of. We didn't have a sheriff, and the town was being bullied by a bunch of ruffians, and nobody wanted the job. We needed somebody willing and able to clean things up. So, they talked Clay into doing it for just a little while. Unfortunately for him, they just kept convincing him to stay on. But now, with all the new folks moving in and the town being pretty calm, he's looked on by many as a ruffian himself. Many of the new folks want him gone. Too bloodthirsty, they say. They weren't here to see how he saved the town back then. But now, I know he agrees with them. He doesn't want the job any more than they want him to have it."

"Well, what does he want?"

Beth slowly lowered her chin and absently turned the sarsaparilla bottle around while she thought about that.

"I don't think even Clay knows at this point. He's drinking himself to death, and he's got something causing him a lot of pain in his belly. I think he just wants to be sixteen again, in the mountains. The mountains he remembers before they came for him."

CHAPTER THREE

Sheriff Clay Brackett pulled his bandana up over his nose and his hat brim farther down to protect his eyes against the stinging sand.

The wind came from the southwest, not unusual in the Owyhee Mountains of Southwest Idaho. The gusts carried with them an assault of tiny particles loosened from the granite to which they had been attached for all-time previous. The shiny grit blew with a rush between

War Eagle Mountain and Florida Mountain, through the streets of Silver City and on down Jordan Creek.

The aged Indian beside him tried to cover his eyes with his arm and stumbled. Brackett tightened his grip on the older man's arm to steady him. The long-lived warrior had injured his neck at some time past, resulting in his head being permanently held at an angle, making him appear to be on the verge of falling sideways as he walked.

"You bring me white man's jail?"

"Yes, Chief."

"How you know I am a chief?"

"You told me so when we first met."

The old warrior snorted as he squinted against the stinging debris pelting his bare chest. He didn't remember ever meeting the young lawman.

"I drink too much? That why you take me white man jail?"

"No. Because you stole Mrs. Yonkers's cat and then tried to sell it back to her."

"I did not know it was her cat when I steal it, or I would not try sell back to her."

"She said the cat was inside her house. How did you get in?"

"Stupid white woman leave window open. I did not know that she have two houses. That one and the store she sells cloth at. When I try sell cat, I did not know the house where the cat lives was her house too. I would not try sell cat to her at store if I know that."

"What else did you take from the house?"

"A fish and one part of pie. She had many fish and would not miss that one little one. I do not think she missed the little piece of pie, too. I hungry. No food. No money to buy food. That why I try sell cat. Not know it was white woman cat or would not try sell it to her. You give food at white man jail?"

"Yeah, Chief, I will give you food."

"That good, give Modoc chief food and chief no more steal white woman cat. How much food you give this chief?"

"You will get supper tonight and breakfast in the morning before you leave the jail."

"Food after that? More food at night again?"

"No, you will be out of jail by then."

The old chief walked along without comment for half a block, running fingers through the white mane of hair, back to where his pigtails started. Without looking directly at the man, Brackett could tell the gears were turning, and another question loomed.

The Chief bent his crooked neck as best he could towards his captor's face. "If I steal more cats, then you feed me more?"

"We should just deal with what we have right now. We can talk about that later."

"We can talk about that later," the chief repeated and then looked up at Brackett again, "When food for Chief?"

Brackett smiled. "Supper will come along when the sun is over there."

He pointed to the southwestern sky. The chief looked where the sheriff indicated and then where the hazy sun lingered, still high in the south.

The chief let out a sigh. "I know where many cats live. Many cats in China Town. Maybe I go there."

Brackett smiled and thought, "This old fellow never stops thinking. Probably why he is still alive."

It hit without warning, just as it always did. Brackett put a hand on his stomach and winced with the burst of pain. The pair walked on for another few feet, and thankfully, the stabbing anguish diminished nearly as fast as it came.

Brackett took a deep breath. "I better give up the drinking before this gets any worse. Maybe next week."

"What say to Chief?"

Brackett hadn't realized he spoke aloud. He straightened himself, steadied the old man, and led the way into the jail. In passing, the sheriff stopped at his desk and picked up a piece of jerky left from the day before. He handed it to the ancient warrior.

"This ought to take the edge off until supper."

The chief began gnawing at it with the side of his jaw where a few usable teeth still resided.

Brackett opened one of the three empty cells and guided the older man inside. "Make yourself to home, Chief."

The chief paid little attention, wholly absorbed in the tasty piece of hard meat, but jumped and whirled around when the iron door clanged shut. His eyes widened; he grabbed ahold of the bars and dropped his jerky. Brackett winced to see a man who had spent his whole life outdoors suddenly trapped like an animal.

"Look here, Chief, how about I leave the door open? I need to have your promise that you will go no farther away than that bench outside on the porch. Can you promise me that?"

"Yes, Yes, Chief promise. Chief just be on bench. No go away."

Brackett unlocked and opened the door. The old man took three quick steps out before turning around, going back into the cell to retrieve the fallen jerky, and then followed the sheriff to a bench on the boardwalk, where he quickly took a seat.

"Remember, you go away, no supper."

"No, no, Chief stay right here on bench on porch."

Brackett patted his prisoner on the shoulder and began rounds of the town.

A quiet Tuesday afternoon, he stopped in at the Idaho Hotel and had a shot of his favorite bourbon with his part-time deputy and the full-time bar manager, Phil. They talked for ten minutes until Phil had to take care of a mine owner and his foreman at the other end of the bar. Brackett left the way he came in. He started through the double doors but stopped to let two of the town's leading ladies pass.

He tipped his hat and said, "Ladies, I hope you are having a fine afternoon."

They didn't acknowledge his courtesy but raised their heads slightly, looking straight ahead. Not untypical. The stories of his gunplay and hard drinking were well known. Most of the city's recently arriving elite felt Silver City, now becoming more sophisticated, should have a sheriff who wasn't so quick to take lives. The pair hustled on down the walk like two geese, their bustles swinging from side to side.

"That boy is no different than those poor men he killed. He showed no mercy or even gave them the benefit of a fair trial," adjudged the more significant and older of the pair as they continued down the street.

"And there's more," said the other, "Why, word has gotten about that he was raised by Indians and might be just as cold-blooded as the ones that continually raid innocent whites."

"Well, they are all savages, you know, and except for his tanned white skin and, I'll admit, extreme good looks, our boy sheriff may be just like the barbarous animals that threaten every traveler."

"Why Mrs. Craig! I'm surprised at you! You should not be noticing his physical attributes. Although they are undeniable." They both giggled as they entered the next store.

Brackett smiled; he knew all of those claims. Phil kept him informed of the local gossip and didn't try to spare the sheriff's feelings. There were times when Sheriff Clay Brackett wondered if the ladies might be closer to right than they suspected.

In the past two years as sheriff, he had added three more bodies to the original six he had dispatched when first he arrived in Silver City. He still felt the sting of finding four white men had savagely murdered his mother and adopted father. The first four he killed in Silver City were those four. Vengeance had never brought satisfaction, but he felt no remorse for the lives he had taken. Even as a teen in the mountains, there had been no sense of anything when he killed. Certainly not remorse or regret. Yes, the ladies probably had a point about him.

The two ladies that stuck their noses in the air were but two of several either coming with their husbands or following them after they got established. They were determined to bring some "civilization and sophistication" to their new community. Their husbands owned, what their peers considered to be, respectable businesses including haberdasheries, general merchandise stores, a jewelry store, a grocery store, and the list grew each month as the silver mines in the mountains continued to pour out their riches.

A dozen of these ladies in the neighborhood consider themselves several paces ahead of the other women of the area. They met for tea and cards and talked of the royals in Russia and England. People they would give anything to emulate. They had read so much about them before bringing their charms to this 'vulgar' place.

None of these women had the slightest idea of what had prompted the gun usage by the sheriff and didn't care to know.

"Maybe it was justified at that time," they commented between sips of tea, "but certainly not now, not in 1868."

"Maybe he did rid the town of the bulk of ruffians, but... that was then and well, now is now," they judged.

"I have been told that he holds a college degree in law and is highly educated," offered one of the group.

"Well! I don't believe that for a moment. Even my husband didn't get to attend a college, and he's on the city council!"

"If he is a college man, why, that would make him nearly the most educated man in this whole worrisome town," returned the first, "I will ask my husband to look into it."

His kind of lawman didn't provide the correct type of image for the town they desired to build. None of them would risk the embarrassment of being caught talking to this young sheriff, this young, well, this young "gunman!"

The majority of those folks had come from big towns east of the Mississippi. The ones arriving from the west coast were less judgmental. Most of them knew all too well the roughness of the west and what it had taken to survive. These Easterners came west not for gold but for business ventures. They had endured the severity of the wagon trains but knew nothing about what it took to start and grow from scratch, a town like Silver City. Most of the miners looked upon them with the same degree of respect given the town's prostitutes. They considered them a necessary leach in the city only to suck in the profits earned by the sweat of the miners' labor. These miners mostly agreed the Eastern merchants did indeed bring a much larger supply of goods with them. But, in the opinion of the miners, the prostitutes were more respectable, far more preferable, and honest.

Brackett smiled, gave a slight shake of his head, and went on down the street the other way. Most of the men who had initially hired him were no longer in office. The mayor continued in his position only because his wife had been the welcoming committee for most new Easterners and saved his mayoral post. Brackett had little support from the new city fathers and doubted he would survive the next election, especially since he had never done anything in the way of campaigning. He had no intention of running again anyway.

He didn't need the money. He had plenty left from his inheritance from relatives he had never met. He had spent little on niceties and still thought more and more about living back in the mountains alone. Yes, the time had to be near.

He walked back to the jail and saw the empty bench.

"Damn!"

He looked up and down the street, hoping the chief had just now decided to take it on the lam. Not seeing the Modoc, he jerked open the door and stopped short. There sat the chief, sitting in the sheriff's chair, feet propped up on the desk, smoking Brackett's last cigar!

"What the hell, Chief! Where did you find that? You been going through my desk?"

The chief took a big pull on the five-inch roll of tobacco, put his head back, and blew out a long stream of smoke.

"HoHo, if I know how good white man smoke, I would have made war many moons ago, just to get this smoke."

CHAPTER FOUR

Minnie Dickerson wiped the sweat from her forehead for what seemed the hundredth time that morning. Being so far from any mining towns and other people made for a lonely life. Not that she had much time for visiting. With a husband and three hungry kids to keep fed, she had a full-time job. Minnie did not have the life her husband had promised when he dragged her west. She longed for the years prior, when their children were aware only of a lovely, although modest, home in Kansas City, Missouri. That simple, safe life all changed when the Union Army's General Thomas Ewing, Jr. issued orders for the detention of any civilians giving aid to William Quantrill's Raiders. Herald Dickerson had provided wood from his mill for Quantrill the month before, and although he didn't think anyone in the town knew about it, he decided to load up his family and get while they could. He never told his wife or kids about supporting the Raiders and publicly held his favor of the North. As a result of his silence, Minnie never could understand why they had to leave their home and business.

Her feelings toward her husband were more dismay and anger than the deep love and respect she had always held for him in most of their years together. As he sat there, using all the proper table etiquette, she somehow faulted him for doing such. He had caused them to be in the middle of Indian wars, mining camps of harsh men and women, danger at every turn. And then, here, he had stuck them. More than three miles from the next household with a woman and children. Farther yet to Silver City, the nearest town of any distinction. He stuck them way up and over a mountain where the timber still grew suitable for his milling.

He could have let them live in the town where she and the children could have had some sense of belonging.

He could have ridden their horse each day to the mill. The distance not much farther than many of the miners traveled each day to and from the mines, and most of them walked. But no! He demanded they live where the only trail consisted of two miles of wagon ruts before it intersected the road to town. Now, here he sat, instructing his children on etiquette while they tried to eat their dinner. As if they would ever get the chance to sit at a white table cloth again or use what he taught. Why didn't he just go ahead and act like the selfish demon he had become? Why put on this disguise as a gentleman? She wanted to spit in his face!

As often happened, she found herself working into a frenzy, and Harold Dickerson would once again be the focus of its fury. Her ire grew as she continued to think of all she had lost.

She no longer had the fashionable dresses in which she had once whirled away the beautiful nights at the church dances. No longer were her hands soft and clean. Her nails were short, broken, and chewed to the quick. She had long since given up on trying to maintain her once beautiful long hair. Now it hung straight and dull, and she had just the day before spotted a grey hair mixed within the blonde. Some days she wondered why she even bothered to spend the five minutes twice a day to brush it out. Five minutes? In Kansas City, she would sit at her dressing table and spend no less than thirty minutes dreamily brushing it until it shone.

"Minnie! What's wrong with you wife? Pay attention. I would think you would pay more cause to me. I'm your husband and father of these fine children."

With a laugh, he reached across the table and ruffled the hair of his teenage daughter. She quickly brought her hand up to re-establish the curls.

"Papa, don't do that! What if young Bill Parsons came along and saw me all amess? Why he'd likely turn around and run off and never marry me. Do you want to be stuck with me forever? Well, do you?"

He chuckled and turned back to his wife, "Me and these two weakling boys of yours have managed to saw up nearly half a wagon load of beams this morning. This afternoon, or there won't be any supper for them; they will help me fill the rest of it. Tomorrow we will take it to Booneville and sell it to Mr. Rodney Stevens in his new saloon. He claims it will be the finest anyplace around. Might even stop in the general store and get you a piece of cloth for you to make a new apron. How would that be? Pretty fine, wouldn't you say?"

He got no answer but a look of profound contempt. He shook his head in bewilderment before turning to his two sons.

"I'll have some of that pie your mama baked this morning. How 'bout you boys?"

Minnie grabbed up the pie tin and dropped it on his plate. He jumped back in shock as she said, "Whatever you demand, husband! You always get what you want, don't you? And I don't need a new apron!"

With that, she strutted to the door and flung it open. But rather than going through it, she found her face buried in the bare stomach of the biggest man she had ever seen. Stunned, she looked up but couldn't see his head looming above the top of the door. She screamed and jumped back.

The behemoth dipped low and still barely made it inside. Once in, the monster stepped aside, and three more normal-sized men entered. They were all dark-skinned, but the cabin dwellers would have been hard-pressed to say whether they were Indian, Mexican, or some combination.

Once the initial shock had worn off, Joshua, the oldest boy, jumped from his chair and started for the rifle hanging over the fireplace.

"I would not do that if I was you, Boy."

The English, spoken by the giant and uttered in a deep, calm voice, froze the boy in his tracks. The huge man turned to Harold Dickerson, still sitting at the table.

"I heard what your woman said to you and how she said it. I don't think she wants to be with you. I'll take her, and she can make pie for us."

At that declaration, Joshua made another go for the gun. The knife, thrown from across the room, lodged into and through his neck. His mother and sister screamed as they started for Joshua's side. The boy's father jumped to his feet, and immediately, the sound of a pistol shot rang out, the ball catapulting Herald Dickinson back against the wall where he clutched at the rapidly growing, bright red spot over his left breast.

In his late teens, Johnny Dickerson, the youngest and most prominent of the children, carried a nearly six-foot muscular frame. He made a gallant leap toward the man who had shot his father. He got his hands around the man's throat, rapidly squeezing the life from the man.

The intruder collapsed to the floor with Johnny holding firm when a colossal hand closed around his own throat. Suddenly, he felt lifted into the air and tossed like a rag doll across the room. He crashed onto the table, but his momentum carried him on across and head first into the hearth of the fireplace, rendering him unconscious.

It would be hours; he didn't know how long for sure before he awakened. He had no hesitation in his thinking and remembering. He quickly listened for a heartbeat on his father and brother. He found none. Ducking into the other two rooms of the house, he found no one. He ran outside shouting for his mother and sister in sheer panic. Far up on the hillside, he could see Horse. Somehow, the savages had missed him. Johnny whistled, and the horse galloped down the hill, hoping for some grain.

CHAPTER FIVE

Brackett heard the shouts even before hearing the pounding footfalls of the horse. He stepped through the jail door to see Johnny Dickerson, Herald Dickerson's youngest son, skidding the lathered-up buckskin to a stop.

"Sheriff, they ran off with Ma and my sister, and they done kilt my daddy and brother!"

Johnny shouted the words through sobs. He bailed out of the saddle and bounded up on the boardwalk.

"How long ago and where?"

"They came right into the house whilst we was havin' dinner! We didn't have a chance! The one they call Bigfoot, I knowd it musta been him, he was there, too."

Brackett got him to sit down on the bench to catch his breath, but the words were pouring out.

"He just stood inside our door and watched. But he speaks good English, he does. Sheriff, we gotta go git Ma and my sister. We gotta go right now!"

"It's after four o'clock. You say they came at noon time?"

"Yes, sir!"

"All right, just settle down for a minute."

"We gotta go right away or...." He didn't finish. Both men knew well enough what the 'or' could mean.

"Look, Johnny, that horse of yours will not make it another mile. Go on over to that big barn up on the next road there. Tell Jackson that I sent you for a good horse and that you will leave the buckskin as collateral. Tell him I will make it right with him later. While you are there, ask him to saddle up my horse and put a pack rig on that brown mule he has. Wait there for me. I will go to the store and get us some grub to keep us for a few days just in case it takes that long."

Johnny went on a run, leading the buckskin behind.

Brackett stuck his head back into the jail and started to say something to the chief, still coveting the cigar. The chief beat him to it.

"White man smoke last a long time."

The sheriff couldn't think of a thing to say, so he just turned around and walked out, leaving the door open. Phil met him at the hitching rail.

"What's all the commotion?"

Brackett filled him in as quickly as he could.

"You're goin' after 'em now? Hell, Clay, it'll be dark in three hours. You best wait till mornin'."

"I am hoping to get a read on which way they are headed. It does not look like rain or snow today, so we can sleep on the trail and have a head start in the morning. Besides, I do not think I can keep that kid from taking off half-cocked. Probably get himself killed if I am not holding him down. Might get himself killed anyway."

He said all this as he walked alongside Phil.

"Might be gone a couple days. Can you keep track of things?"

"Yep, been so quiet lately I doubt I'll be needed. I'll go back to the jail and keep track of your cat-stealing renegade."

Brackett gave him a nod and a brief wave and stepped into The Eatery café, where he found Mayor Drew Bongenhielm and one of the new city councilmen. He explained what he intended to do, and Phil would be in charge in his absence. Phil assured him all would be well.

The new councilman objected to leaving the town without its sheriff for several days, but the mayor set him straight.

"These are residents of the county, and it's his job to try to save 'em."

"Well, I don't like it. Not a bit. I'll be talkin' it over with the other councilmen."

The mayor sighed, "You do that, Henry. You do that."

With that, the councilman stood up, and tossing his napkin on his empty plate, walked out. The mayor looked at Brackett and shrugged.

"These new folks just don't understand yet. They will after they been here for a while, but you and I will probably not have our jobs by then."

"Well, I can live with being out of work, Mayor. Thanks for standing up for me, though."

"Be careful, Clay. And good luck."

Bethany Alexander came out of the kitchen, wiping her hands on her apron.

"Hello, Clay. Didn't see you for breakfast or dinner today."

"I had to go round up a cat thief."

"A cat thief? Sounds dangerous."

Brackett smiled and held up his hands to indicate that he wasn't up to the mental combat she would undoubtedly win.

"Any chance you could throw together some lunch for two? I am going out of town for a few days but would sure like to start out with a belly full of your good cooking."

"No time to just sit and eat for a moment?"

"Not right now, Beth. There is a kid out there waiting for me. Indians got away with his mother and sister. Guess I will need to find them."

"Oh no! I'll get started, just a few minutes."

"No need to hurry. I need to go to my room to get my possibles and then to the store to gather some goods for several days out. I will work on that while you make up the lunches. Probably take a good twenty or thirty minutes."

CHAPTER SIX

Brackett found no way to convince Johnny he needed to stay behind and nurse the lump on his head. The boy's grit and determination reminded Brackett of himself at a similar age. He found the boy sitting on the dirt outside Jackson's Stable. He straightened up as soon as he saw Brackett.

"Horses and mule is ready, Sheriff. Can we go now?"

"Johnny, I still think I would have a better chance alone. How about staying here?"

"Sheriff, if it was jist reglar Injuns that took ma and sis, I might let you go it alone. But yer gonna need some help up against that monster, Bigfoot!"

Brackett didn't respond to that. He got on board Pluto and led the mule to the general store, where they loaded the animal's pack with food and other supplies. The image of Nampuh did not keep his thoughts on the renegade tribe. In his mind, he saw the one they called Dark Coyote. His boyhood friend, Knife Thrower.

Some claimed all the stories of a huge, renegade Indian were nothing more than that. Just stories. Brackett knew better. During the past few years, he had talked with many Paiutes, Shoshonis, and Bannacks, who roamed the mountains and deserts of Southern Idaho, Northern Utah, and Northern Nevada.

None of them wanted anything to do with Owlux or, as many called him, Nampuh. The name referred to his oversized feet. He had once been the leader of a large Bannack band, but Col. George Crook had wiped out most of his braves in December of 1866 on the Owyhee River, and then the vengeful officer had pursued the rest to Steens Mountain where nearly all bunch were either killed or captured. Some said Howluck headed the outfit, but Brackett didn't believe that.

Brackett knew of Howluck. He, too, had the reputation of being large in stature and being one of the most dangerous Indian leaders. Often, folks argued about who committed the atrocities against white travelers, Howluck or Nampuh. Large moccasin tracks were found when either was in the area.

Nampuh had somehow escaped and was now believed to be nothing more than the leader of a bunch of outcasts. His renegades were known to kill for no apparent reason. Area tribes offered the outlaws no refuge and, as a result, were just as nervous about them as the whites. Many of his conversations about the man with tribal leaders told why the giant and his followers were so ruthless. Most agreed he had been raised by Cherokees on their reservation and educated by white teachers who forbade the speaking of native languages. Folks believed, "he was good with his book learnin', and he is one smart Indian, or whatever you want to call him."

Explanations of how he came to the Owyhee Mountains and surrounding high deserts varied. Just the week before, Joan Blackbird, married to a foreman of one of the more productive mines, told Brackett what she knew of the story.

"He left the nation because of his temper. Growing up, he got teased about his size. He almost killed a couple young men and fled to avoid prosecution. My cousin, Sweetbird, was living there when it happened. She said the reservation leaders got him hired onto a wagon train headed to Oregon. When he wanted to, he could be very nice and was very good-looking. Sweetbird said Nampuh's father was white and his mother a blend of negro and Cherokee. She said he could make a person forget about his size with his easy laugh and broad smile. But she also said she had seen him change in an instant when he thought someone was laughing at him. She said he is very smart and got good grades."

They were sitting on Joan Blackbird's front porch. Joan in her rocking chair, smoking the ever-present corncob pipe. Joan had also been well educated in California's white man's school and sent there by the great Paiute chief of the time for that reason. Now she acted as a translator from time to time with the Army. Well respected by Paiutes, Shoshonis, and Bannacks, the Army paid Joan well for her services and cared for her when she traveled with them.

She took another puff and continued, "Somewhere along the Snake River, down below here, the wagon train stopped for the night. Nampuh had fallen hard for a pretty white girl while driving her families' wagon. I guess the old man was stove up or something. Anyway, the girl had led him to believe the feelings were mutual. All that was good until this artist fella joined the train and immediately took to the girl. The girl was swept off her feet by the smooth-talker and was just polite but cold to Nampuh after that. Well, it came to pass that while they were stopped for the night, this artist and Nampuh, by the way, his real name is Wilkinson, Starr Wilkinson. Named by his father after some distant cousin or some such that had a reputation as an outlaw in the Midwest. The way Nampuh was said to tell it later, this artist and Nampuh were gathering firewood along the river, and Starr, err, Nampuh, says to him that the girl is his and he's going to marry her when they get to Oregon. At this, the artist makes a big mistake. He laughs and says something like: Did Nampuh really think she would pick an overgrown black man over a good-looking fella like him. Well, Nampuh says if the guy says it again, he'll break him in half and toss his sorry ass in the river."

Joan took another pull on the corncob and then a swig from a bottle of Brackett's favorite bourbon, brought for her and her husband. Going after the stuff as she did, Brackett had to wonder if there would be any left when Cliff got home that evening.

"So, what happened then?"

"Oh, yeah, well, the artist made his second mistake. He up and pulled a little pistol from his fancy vest and threatened to shoot Nampuh if he tried anything. Well, that sure enough upset the big boy, and he started after the artist. The shot went into his side, but that just made him madder."

"Never heard no more of what Nampuh had to say about what happened next, but what is known, Nampuh came back from the river, and the artist never did. They searched for him but never found a body. The folks on the wagon train figured Nampuh had killed him and thrown his carcass in the river. The girl was upset and wouldn't even talk to Nampuh. She called him a murderer. Told him to never come near to her again. The leaders of the train voted to throw him out, and he left and headed into these mountains where he hooked up with a band of Paiutes and kinda took over."

Joan stood up and said she'd be back. She disappeared around the corner to the outhouse. Brackett stood up and walked to the middle of the road to stretch his legs. He knew he should be making the rounds of the town, but hooked on the story unwinding for him, he walked back up on the porch and took a swig of the bourbon just as Joan resumed her position on the rocking chair.

"I'll tell you something, young Sheriff, I sure do like this firewater you bring to me and Cliff. But you keep hittin' it like you just done, well, you sure will need to bring me some more to make up for it."

"Well, you keep educating me on these legends, and I will keep bringing you these bottles. But you better go easy on that firewater yourself because Cliff will beat you if you do not save him some for after supper. Cannot say I would blame him."

They both laughed, and she took another swig and re-lit the pipe.

"Now, where was I?"

"They ran Nampuh off, and he had taken up with a band of Paiutes up here somewhere."

"That's right. Well, it was late fall, and the wagon train moved on for a couple days but decided to winter right down there by where the ferry crosses now. Early the next spring, Nampuh and his bunch were hungry after a long winter, and they happened onto the wagon train. Well, at first, Nampuh didn't realize that it was the same train. He figured they had gone on to Oregon. But as the band was set on steeling two or three head of cattle and got closer, he recognized the brands on the cattle, and that's when he figured out that it was the train that had kicked him out. He then rounded up the cattle as planned and brought them away to slaughter later on. But, the more he thought about that train, the more it ate at him."

"Story goes that he later told how he convinced his band of about 40 or 50 raiders that they could take everything. So, they just went back down, killed nearly everybody, including the girl. After that, they did several more raids, and that's when that Colonel Crook took after him. Course, that's just a combination of stories I've heard and kinda put together."

"You think it is mostly true?"

"The first part is. My cousin knew that part straight up. The last part? I don't know. Makes sense why he's so mean. From what I know of a couple others in his bunch, they have their own reason for hating white people. The one they call the Dark Coyote is said to be the worst. Matter fact, I hear that he was part of the tribe that you grew up in. They used to call him Knife Thrower."

CHAPTER SEVEN

Brackett did a final inspection of the pack on the mule and told Johnny to go ahead. He would catch up. Stepping into Plato's saddle, the sheriff rode the big Andalusian stud to the jail's front entrance, where his part-time deputy sat on the bench. Phil looked up from the stick he'd been carving.

"Got everything you need, Boss?"

"I think so. How about you? You be all right while I am gone? I should have hired January Yanni as our full-time deputy when I had the chance. Now it is just you and me. What does your real boss say about you taking time from the saloon?"

Plato stomped once as his patience began to diminish and put an exclamation point on it by slapping the mule with his tail. The mule backed off a step.

"Oh, he's all right. He put Miss Divine behind the bar. She was happy to have a break from her uh, usual duties. She won't make as much money, but I think she's beginning to tire of the life upstairs anyway."

"All right then, I will be taking my leave. Oh, by the way, you can let the Chief go on his way any time now. Make sure he gets some food to take with him. I promised him breakfast tomorrow."

"You're a bit late on that one. Left a few minutes ago. Kind of upset when I told him there wouldn't be any supper for him tomorrow. I fed him supper a while ago, and Beth gave him enough food to keep him for a day, or maybe two if he goes easy on it. By the way, I charged it to your tab at Beth's place."

"Of course, you did. You know the city is supposed to pay for that stuff."

"I know, but if I charge it to the city, I have to sign for it. Don't have to do that if I just tell Beth to put it on your tab. Anyhow, I figure you can fill out one of them papers you use to get it back from the mayor."

"How was the chief when he left, knowing he does not get to sleep in a bed tonight?"

"Grouchy, I think. How the hell do you know one way or the other with them injuns? I think he was happy with the food, but he slumped outta here mumbling something about cats in China Town."

Brackett dropped his chin to his chest and smiled. He heard Phil chuckle. With a salute to his deputy, he turned Plato into the street and headed after Johnny Dickerson.

"Johnny, I sure wish you would let me take on this pursuit alone. I can move faster if I do not have to be concerned about you."

"Dontcha worry none 'bout me, Sheriff. I been all over these mountains, and I got me this here rifle. Just bought it from the store, and I got me a whole box of lead to push through it if'n I need it. And I knowd how to use it, too. I been the one bringin' in the game for my family for more'n two years now. Come on, Sheriff, you ain't but a few years older'n me no how. Let's get on with gittin' my mama and sis back."

Brackett thought no advantage could be attained in arguing. And, who could know, maybe the boy might be more capable than he looked. Certainly determined and no quit in him. Of that, Brackett could be sure.

Johnny, the mule in tow, trotted ahead. A few minutes later, Johnny started across the creek and up toward his cabin. Brackett called to him, and with irritation, he trotted back.

"What's the matter, Sheriff? Ain't we gonna track 'em from our homestead?"

"Thought we might have a better chance of intercepting the bunch if we head directly toward where they are most likely going."

Even though the Dickerson cabin set back up the mountain, Joan Blackbird told him just a few days earlier that if someone wished to catch up with Nampuh when on the run, they most likely would need to head southwest toward South Mountain. There were, as of yet, few roads and trails leading off in that direction. Brackett decided to strike out in a more direct route to cut the course of the kidnappers. He had no idea of the kind of horses the bunch would be riding, but he knew there would be one unmistakable sign. Giant human footprints mixed in with the hoofprints.

Brackett explained to Johnny his reasoning and what Joan Blackbird had told him during the first mile. Johnny seemed somewhat skeptical but agreed to follow along. Brackett led the way up, away from Jordan Creek, and eventually on top of a long ridge from where they got their first look at South Mountain in the distance. Snow already topped the peak.

Might be a warning of a hard winter, thought Brackett. It brought back memories of his childhood when two different times, Buha, his adopted father and leader of the Indian clan that raised the white child, had gotten caught off guard. Both times, the tribe had made it down to their wintering grounds at the confluence of the Owyhee River at the Snake. They had made it only after great suffering on the long trek.

For a while, Brackett and Johnny were able to follow the wagon road, built as a toll road a couple of years before by a man named Skinner. Finally, they left the road and started up and down the steep hillsides where they wound back and forth, switchback after switchback. Long and tedious but better than wearing out the horses right off the bat. They rode in silence with only the sounds of squeaking leather and horseshoes striking rocks. Johnny had wrapped the mule's lead rope around his saddle horn, and Brackett could hear the boy's frustration when the mule failed to keep the pace.

While riding out of a gulch onto the mountain proper, Brackett's mind kept going back to what Joan Blackbird had told him, "The one they call the Dark Coyote is one of the worst. In fact, I hear that he was part of the tribe that you grew up in. They used to call him Knife Thrower."

Brackett knew why his childhood friend would be vindictive after watching his village, mother, young brother and sisters, being brutalized and finally murdered by the four white men who also killed Brackett's mother and adopted father. Brackett, too, had lost his half-brothers and sisters. He tried to think what he would be like if he hadn't been able to gain some satisfaction of vengeance. Or, what if he had not spent those years with the whites to understand the pale skins were not all animals. Knife Thrower had no opportunity for any of that. But still, he had a hard time picturing Knife Thrower being so full of hate he would commit such atrocities on people who had nothing to do with the massacre of his family. And yet, according to Joan, there were no doubts about it, Dark Coyote and Knife Thrower, the same person. Dark Coyote! A name that would suggest the worst of a human being.

CHAPTER EIGHT

Dark Coyote, still seething at not being allowed to kill the woman and girl at the cabin, had no thoughts other than destroying every white who dared venture into his mountains. Let them stay in their camps, looking for gold and silver, but let him punish all bold enough to stray. He especially didn't want a single one of these intruders setting up their camps or houses in the hills, he still claimed. Along with their men, this woman and girl had committed that sin. They built their log lodge within a mile of where he had grown up. He wanted to leave a message for any who might follow. A statement showing what would happen if they tried to come to that area ever again. He felt little enough satisfaction with simply killing the man and boys. He wanted the whites to see even their women were not safe.

But, Nampuh would not allow it. The big Indian? Indian? At this thought, Dark Coyote scoffed under his breath. Indian? Nampuh did not appear to him to be Indian at all. Some mix of white and black, he thought. Looked more white than black. Not Indian, though.

His thoughts returned to the cabin. Nampuh had grabbed his wrist before he could plunge his knife into the woman. He sat straddled across her as she screamed. His arm fully extended above his head. His hand clutching the blade, and just as he started down with it, he felt his wrist jerked back so forcefully that the knife flew from his fingers, and he fell onto his back. When he looked up, Nampuh stood over him. With the unmistakable look so many had come to dread, he stared down Dark Coyote and slowly waved one finger back and forth. Enraged, Dark Coyote jumped to his feet and started again for the woman. He took only one step before being knocked a full body length to the ground by a backhand.

He looked at Nampuh, who reached down and pulled the woman to her feet. With that, the woman and girl were tied onto their plow horse, and the band started away. Dark Coyote swore an oath to himself. He would get revenge for the way Nampuh had treated him.

He had now been with the band of renegades for over a year and felt he deserved far more respect. He had killed more whites than any others, yet beyond his understanding, they still treated him like an outsider and ridiculed him for killing small children and women. They didn't seem to understand. The only means by which the Indian way of life could be salvaged would come by injecting so much fear in the minds of the whites they would eventually leave. He felt like the others were not genuinely motivated for the same pure reasons prompting his actions. Of course, they weren't all Indians, either. Some were Mexicans, and some he couldn't be sure what they were. Half-breeds, he thought. He felt disgusted by their desire to accumulate white man possessions. Even Nampuh, whom at first he had admired, seemed to be caught up in taking white man plunder.

The band rode along behind Nampuh, who always led the way with his gigantic strides and seeming determination to reach a destination he rarely revealed to his followers. Minnie Dickerson and her teenage daughter tried to stay centered on the bareback work horse. The animal, seldom ridden, had an uncomfortable, jostling gait. Its big feet jolted its riders with every step. Minnie had only the mane to hang on to and Mercy, the girl, had only her mother's waste for security. Clutching the animal with their legs helped stabilize them, but it also caused their legs to cramp. One of the captors led the horse. Their feet and hands were no longer tied, but no doubt remained in their minds. They could not get away.

"Mama, what will they do with us?" whispered Mercy.

"I don't know. Hush up now."

Her warning came too late, and once again, the long lance-like stick carried by the rider behind them slammed into the girl's right shoulder. Her painful protest brought another whack. This time she bit her lip and kept quiet. She rubbed her shoulder as more tears streamed down an already dust-streaked face.

Although he told them nothing, all the men knew they were headed for a winding, sharp-sided gulch on the far side of the great inselberg the white man called South Mountain. At the bottom of the gulley ran a year-round stream. It would take the better part of three days for most folks to make the journey over the nearly impassable terrain, but they knew Nampuh not to be *most folks*. Moving at a steady pace, they would be there in less than 24 hours. Weather permitting, they might not even stop for darkness. He never slowed, never speeded up, never faltered. He just continued on and on, hour after hour. He didn't stop to rest. When coming across a creek or spring, he would flop onto his massive chest and drink. Less than a minute later, he would be up and striding out once more. The rest of his band would have to stop from time to time to rest the horses. When this happened, he would keep going. He would be waiting for them at the gorge, having arrived well ahead.

CHAPTER NINE

Clay Brackett tried to be civil with Johnny Dickerson but found his patience growing thin with the kid riding next to him questioning everything from stopping to water the horses to which side of a ridge they should take.

He understandably wanted to find his mother and sister but had not one bit of knowledge of how Bigfoot and his followers would travel. Brackett could not be certain himself but felt pretty sure he knew where they were going. After sixteen years of living and hunting in these mountains as a young man, Clay Brackett knew where every creek and water hole ran in what had become known as the Silver City Range. He found his memory of South Mountain vaguer.

Suddenly, he felt an uncontrollable rage at his young companion. The gun barrel between Johnny's eyes brought the boy to silence.

"You have three choices. Shut the hell up, go on by yourself or take a bullet right here between your beady little eyes."

He shoved the end of the barrel harder into the kid's forehead.

"What you do not get to do is say one more thing about what I am doing. What is your choice?"

The anger abated as quickly as it appeared, and Brackett pulled the gun away and rode forward. Johnny sat still for a full minute, watching the young sheriff ride away. He weighed his options and decided Brackett had made his point. The boy didn't fully understand what he had said to bring on the outburst but would watch how and what he said in the future. He gave a tug on the mule and touched his spurs to his mount.

Prospectors found gold on the west side of South Mountain and put up a small town named after the mountain on which it rested. There were too many people in South Mountain City, and Brackett felt Bigfoot would not choose to camp nearby. Nampuh and Dark Coyote would take the women to a creek Brackett had visited a couple of times in his youth. On the East side. They wouldn't get down to business with the women until they reached their destination. Then? Well, that question from Johnny he chose not to answer.

"I thought you said South Mountain. Well, there it is. Why don't we just go straight for it? Why are we wandering off to the side of it like we're adoin'?" Johnny caught his attitude and quickly added. "Not complaining, you understand. Just askin'."

"It is a big mountain, and they will not be going to the west side."

Somehow, his question hadn't seemed to bother the sheriff, and he sighed in relief. He needed to be more careful.

The kid swore something under his breath and then out loud at the mule. He kicked his horse and jerked the mule's lead rope to catch up with Brackett.

As he pulled alongside Plato's hind quarters, he asked, "How do you know that? Have you been here before?"

Brackett didn't look back but did give a short answer, "A couple times. Just a guess, but I think I am right. Too many people over on the west side."

Johnny thought to himself but knew better than to say it aloud, "Well, yer aguessin' with the lives of my kin, and I don't like it!"

Brackett saw the doubt in the kid's face and could feel an uncontrollable fit of anger coming on. It took all of him to keep it inside.

With a touch of the rein, Plato stopped. Johnny moved beside as Brackett stepped down and hooked the left stirrup on the saddle horn. Loosening the cinch, he shifted the blanket and saddle while working on getting his temper back in check. Finally, he re-tightened the cinch.

In the saddle again, he looked at Johnny.

"I think it might be better if you go your own way. I will do the best I can to get your mother and sister back. Who knows, doing it your way, you might find them first. The straightest way to the mountain is up over that ridge. You go ahead and take the mule. As I remember, you will come to a small stream at the bottom of the gulley. Will not be much water in it this time of the year, but you should be able to fill your water pouch and get a good drink for you and the animals. I will be going this other way. There is plenty of food for you and even for your mother and sister if you find them."

He clicked his tongue, and Plato moved ahead. Johnny said nothing but watched as Brackett disappeared over a slight rise.

The boy surveyed his surroundings and shaded his eyes as he looked to the west. Sunset would be soon and had already gotten a lone coyote to sing somewhere in the dusk. He suddenly had the loneliest feeling in his young life. Never before had he been so completely alone. He had never spent a night away from his family. Suddenly, grief and anger overcame everything else, and he realized his best hope would be with Brackett. He spurred the horse into a gallop across the rocky ground and over the ridge. Within ten minutes, he caught up with Brackett.

"There won't be no more complaints or questioning from me."

Brackett nodded but didn't answer. The east side of South Mountain lay over ridge after ridge until a great basin finally laid out before them. With the light fading and the first stars visible, Brackett stopped at a stream to water the horses and mule and fill his water bag.

"Are we gonna stop for the night?"

"No, we will continue on. From what I know of Nampuh, he will keep going until he reaches his camp. But they will have to stop and rest their horses just as we do. They would have followed Jordan Creek until it intersected with Flint Creek and then up over the mountains like we have. But we have gained the advantage of going straight across from Silver City. We may have picked up as much as three hours on their head start."

Brackett pulled a flask from his saddle bags and took a long pull on its contents. He re-capped it and tossed it to Johnny. Johnny removed the cap and took a whiff.

"What in tarnation is that? It smells horrible."

Brackett took back the flask, "It is bourbon and a good version of it, too. Not a drinker, I would guess?"

"Never even smelled it before."

"Well, that is probably a good thing," he said and took one more sip before reinstalling it in his saddle bag.

Both mounted up again, and Brackett took a look at the stars, glad to see the slight glare in the East, promising a full moon within half an hour.

"I would guess we can reach the creek I am headed for by midnight."

They would need a lot of luck to find the encampment that night, but Brackett determined they would try. The coyote sang out again, and the mule joined the choir with its bray.

Brackett found the creek he sought. It ran lower than remembered, but that should be expected given the time of year. The moon traversed from the east to the southern sky until shedding light to benefit both the hunted and the hunters. Undecided which way to follow the creek, Brackett hesitated. Going back down in an eastern direction would be more accessible, but he figured up the stream made more sense. Nampuh would undoubtedly be secluded in an easy-to-guard notch on the mountainside. Brackett decided to pull back a half-mile or so and then parallel the creek looking for tracks, not wanting to run head-on into an ambush. If he and Johnny could cross the trail to their hiding place, it would give them a chance to do some scouting. Maybe they could avoid blundering into a scrimmage they could not win.

CHAPTER TEN

They had gone no more than half a mile when a cloud crept over the moon, taking away all the light. A rumble in the distance now made it obvious, a storm headed toward them, and the night would soon turn cold, wet, and windy. A slight break in the clouds gave Brackett a chance to look around and pick out a stand of aspens growing up against a north-facing wall of granite. With the storm coming in from the southwest, this north face would offer some protection from the wind. They were too far from the creek to obtain water, but with some quick effort, they could cut enough leafy limbs from the aspens to create a shelter of sorts, and with luck, perhaps there would even be a bit of overhang from the rock that could keep some rain off.

As the increasing clouds passed by, the two men found their way to the grove and up to the rampart of nature's making. While Johnny hacked away at limbs with his skinning knife, Brackett made his way along the face of the wall until satisfied with the overhang he found. An indentation deep enough to keep the two men and their riggings dry. With the limbs placed vertically in front of the opening, they could have a small fire and yet not have it seen. The little smoke produced would be dispersed through the leaves. The horses and mule would not have it so good. They would have to weather the storm with only the protection the grove would give.

As Brackett placed the last branch, lightning lit up the night, and a thunderclap followed almost immediately. Brackett walked to the horses and held Plato's nose, whispering to the warhorse, reassuring it. Johnny ran a rope around several trees to form a small corral. As another precaution, he and Brackett used lead ropes to hobble the animals, just in case they should break out of the rope corral during the night.

They sat and ate the lunch Beth had made for them. Several slabs of roast beef, rolls, freshly made that morning, a couple baked spuds, no butter but salted and peppered, and finally, they unwrapped a paper containing two-quarter slices of apple pie. They ate much of it, but with Johnny's worries and Brackett's stomach problems, there remained enough for a big breakfast.

The raindrops started lightly and grew heavier as the wind hissed and then roared through the grove. Brackett laid back against his saddle as the little fire played images across the top and side of the shelter and listened to the storm beyond. He could hear the horses stomping once in a while, but they didn't sound nervous. Three feet away, he sensed Johnny, facing away on his side, wept. The boy had lost his father and brother and didn't know if his mother and sister were even alive, and if alive, perhaps dealing with horrors worse than death. Brackett knew the feeling of losing his parents but couldn't think of anything to say that might offer some comfort.

The cave lit up! Brighter than what the sun would give. At the same time, thunder cracked like a thousand bullwhips. The grove burst into flame, on fire from the lightning strike. Brackett and Johnny were instantly on their feet, tearing away the aspen bows already on fire.

Plato gave forth a scream and bolted from the grove, tearing away the rope corral even though hobbled. The other horse and the mule were not so fortunate. They had been struck dead with the lightning and lay smoldering in the inferno. Brackett grabbed his rifle and hat and guided Johnny along the stone face until they were clear of the flames. The rain continued to come in great waves, and soon the grove smoldered in the center where the lightning had set it afire. Within another ten minutes, the ground became cool and muddy.

As more lightning flashed, lighting up everything for a mile in every direction, Brackett scanned the area for any sign of Plato. Had the scream been one of fear or one of agony? Brackett had never before heard anything like that from the big horse. The aspen copse had been reduced to half its original size, and seeing nothing of the horse during each lightning flash, Brackett knew Plato had gotten away, not lingering nearby. As the storm moved on and the lightning flashes were too far away to help see, Brackett went back to the cavern. Some coals still showed red and yellow indications of heat. Johnny joined

Brackett and fed the fire with dry sticks from back of the overhang. There remained nothing to be said. Johnny knew they were not only farther from finding his mother and sister but farther from being able to save themselves. With the fire restored, nothing remained to do but wait for dawn.

Brackett shook his head, trying to clear the fog and trying to remember what happened the night before. Slowly, everything began to come back into focus. He cursed himself for the weakness.

The two walked out of the cave before sunrise. Brackett strained to see some indication of the passing band of renegades. Indeed, if they had not passed before the storm, the likelihood of tracks left in the mud should be good. On the other hand, if they had beaten the storm, there would be little left.

All the time, as they walked, he kept looking into the distance in hopes of seeing Plato. He knew the big Andalusian would have come back to him if he could. The fact he had not concerned him deeply. He tried to concentrate on finding the tell-tale tracks.

Mid-morning brought no new sign of any horses crossing the creek. Johnny had been silent all morning, and that suited Brackett just fine. There seemed not one good thing he could say to the kid. Johnny labored, having a hard time keeping up because of the heavy work boots. Brackett left his boots with his other gear at the cave, where they spent the night in exchange for his moccasins. With the sheriff getting farther and farther ahead, Johnny finally called out.

"Hey there! Can ya hold up there?"

Brackett stopped and waited as he surveyed the landscape ahead. The creek had disappeared behind a long, low ridge, half a mile distant. He had been in this area when not more than thirteen years old. Buha, his Indian stepfather, had brought him along with ten warriors on an elk hunt. For more than a week, they had explored around the mountain. He shook his head at not being able to remember all the details of the creeks. He thought this one stayed near the base before finally diving sharply away back to the east and into a canyon where it fed a larger body of water. But he could be remembering an altogether different stream. He began thinking he made a mistake by not going downstream instead of up. They could turn back and be back to the cave by midday and then strike out for the lower areas of the mountain. Doing that now would leave them unsure if they had made the right decision.

"I'm havin' me a hell of a time keepin' the pace," Johnny said as he came huffing and puffing.

Brackett made no return comment but pointed to the ridge. "I think we should walk over that ridge and make sure where we are in regards to the creek. It could be that we need to turn around and go back downstream. I might not be right about where they are headed. I have seen no sign."

"We might not find 'em, huh?" said Johnny, his head looking at his shoelaces. The words were so quiet Brackett barely caught them.

"I cannot say, Johnny, but I can tell you that if we give up, we for sure will not find them. You ready?"

"Yes, sir. I'll try harder to keep up."

Brackett nodded and took the first steps toward the ridge. He could hear Johnny laboring behind him. Half an hour later, they topped the rise, and Brackett cussed.

"Damn, the creek doubled back on us. We have been walking in the wrong direction for two hours!"

"What'll we do?"

The familiar pain began building again in Brackett's gut, producing a grunt. He sat down on a rock, bending over his knees with agony.

"We go back the way we came, but this time we will keep the creek in sight."

"You all right?"

"Yes. Just give me a minute."

CHAPTER ELEVEN

It had been an endless night for the Dickerson women. When the storm hit, they were tied back-to-back under a juniper tree to wait it out. Twice, lightning had struck within a hundred yards of where they sat. The tree offered little protection from the cold, soaking rain. They shivered so intensely Minnie thought they would both surely perish of the cold.

When they were finally untied and jerked to their feet at dawn, they both collapsed from stiffness. Instantly they were slapped across the back of their heads and again yanked to their feet. Both tried with every ounce of strength they could muster to stay upright. Minnie widened her stance and leaned on the tree to steady herself, but Mercy attempted to take a short step and crumpled to the ground again. This time the captor took hold of her long hair and began dragging her twenty feet to the workhorse. She grabbed his wrist and held it tight to take some of the pressure off her hair. Her screams brought more slaps and a kick to her midsection.

Dark Coyote had wanted to kill the women to start with, and now it became his job to care for them. If he couldn't kill them, he would see that they wished for death. He delighted in seeing the mother in panic for her daughter. In them, he saw the white men that had killed his sisters and mother. His mourning had turned to a great sense of loss and then to an ever-growing hatred for all white people. Now, he burned with a desire to cause every kind of pain possible to as many whites as possible. For now, these two white women would suffer until he could kill them.

Clay Brackett and his mother were the only white people he had ever known. The mother had been killed simultaneously as his own, and Brackett had returned to the white man's world. Now, the boy that had been his best friend in their youth lived among the whites, and he, Dark Coyote, would show him no more mercy than any other of his kind.

He pulled the girl to her feet by her dress top, and it ripped, exposing her shoulder. She shrieked again, and he slapped her across her face as a reward. By then, the adrenalin had kicked in for Minnie, and she rushed to her daughter. Stumbling and falling halfway and rising again, she attacked Dark Coyote with the vengeance of a mother bear protecting its cub.

The woman's fingernails were in his eye before he could block the assault. Too late, he let go of the girl and threw the mother away from him. She ripped his right eye from his head, so it dangled there by a bloody strand.

He stumbled away in silent agony, trying in vain to put the eyeball back into the open socket. Finally, he ripped it loose and threw it aside. Blood poured over his chest. In shock, the total pain had not yet taken its toll, but he felt complete in his sheer rage. With his left hand covering the place that had once held his right eye, he searched for the woman. When he saw her holding her daughter as they both huddled on the ground, he pulled out his knife and swung at the woman's face. The blade took off the back of Minnie's scalp as she ducked just in time to prevent her throat from being cut. The scream of Dark Coyote came not from pain but instead from an inner storm beyond description. The racking, throbbing anguish suddenly hit him, and he doubled over with it while still swinging the knife wildly without seeing a target. Minnie knew she had been cut badly, but her need to protect her daughter overcame all other demands, and she jumped to her feet, pulling Mercy with her. They hobbled to the other side of the horse to escape the knife blade. Nampuh put his hand on her shoulder from behind. When she turned toward him, she knew he would kill her.

"Woman! Stop! He will hurt you no more. Behave yourselves. You will be free of this bunch soon."

Shock filled Minnie! He talked in English as if it were his first language! As she looked at him, she saw he didn't look like the other Indians or Mexicans making up his band of murderers.

"What do you want with us? Why have you taken us?"

"I plan on selling you back to the whites. They will pay for your return."

"You killed my family. There is no one to pay."

Instantly, she knew she had made a potentially fatal mistake in admitting no one remained to pay a ransom.

"Perhaps, perhaps not. If that be the case, then I will sell you to the Mexican slavers. Makes no difference to me. The thing you need to know is that I want you alive and well. You're no good to me dead. So, I will protect you and your daughter until I find a buyer."

He lifted her onto the workhorse and then Mercy behind her. She looked down from the horse to the other side, desperately hoping the knife of Dark Coyote didn't still slash through the air. She found him nowhere in sight.

Minnie's scalp, a third the size of the palm of her hand, hair still attached, dangled from the back of her head. With much tenderness, Mercy replaced the blood-soaked scalp where it had been severed. She tore off the bottom of her long dress and wrapped it around her mother's bleeding head. The pain in Minnie's scalp felt close to unbearable, but she could do nothing about that. She tried to stay silent both for her daughter and for fear of being punished even more. Once in a while, a whimper or low groan would slip from her lips, and she would desperately look about for the blows that had followed previous sounds. She looked for the man who wielded the knife, but he didn't seem to be with the band anymore.

She watched the giant man, the group's apparent leader, walking away from the camp even as the others hurriedly gained their horses or began trudging along behind. Mercy whispered to her mother what she heard. The outlaw group called him Nampuh, and now, as the day before, he struck out ahead of the horses. His stride and endurance seemed to outdo the walking paces of the horses that followed.

"What did he mean when he said he might sell us to Mexican slavers, Mama?"

"I don't know, Mercy, be quiet now."

They rode on for another hour, receiving none of the harsh punishment they had received from Dark Coyote. The pain seemed to be diminishing a little with the scalp laid back in place, and Minnie found herself thinking of how they might escape. Far from educated in the way of Indians or Mexicans, still, she knew the word *slave* and what it had always meant to those subjected to it. Everybody had seen how many negros were treated in Missouri even after the war. She could imagine what two white women would be subjected to in such a world. The fear for her daughter raged so strong she gave little thought to her own salvation. She just knew that first, they must survive, and secondly, they must escape.

CHAPTER TWELVE

Johnny had walked in silent contemplation, but then he spoke solemnly, “If they are still alive, they’ve probably been bad mistreated.”

Brackett didn’t answer. Another mile up the creek, and again Johnny spoke.

“Even if we find ‘em, they won’t never be the same. They most likely been beaten and raped. Raped by Indians and Mexicans and whatever that big one is.”

Again, Brackett kept walking without comment. He didn’t like where Johnny’s thoughts were taking the kid, but he couldn’t deny the truth in his words. He also knew whatever Nampuh’s reason for taking the woman and girl, it had nothing to do with a kind heart. He had something in mind for them. Unlike most Indian bands raiding settlers and miners, this renegade band rode only for profit. They wanted gold and silver as much as the miners who dug for it.

They didn't take usable goods from those they killed. They took the money, gold, silver, jewelry, and, of course, guns and ammunition—much the same as road agents in any country. The difference in this band, they also took women and children. Brackett felt confident they didn't just take them for their own pleasures but for profit. Several tribes would gladly trade goods for white women and children, but they would not offer what Nampuh's outfit looked to find. He knew white captives had been sold back to their own families but only on rare occasions. Also, they had no way of knowing Johnny lived and could only assume they killed these women's family. Most likely the only ones that might have paid a ransom.

Brackett believed if the women cooperated, they would not be killed. He also knew being kept alive might be a curse. He had heard of women after being rescued from Indians. Some had their tongues cut out. Some had been branded or tattooed on their faces. Some came back insane. He briefly wondered if Johnny had heard these stories.

He thought of his mother, how differently she and her baby had been treated. Buha had adopted him and raised him. Buha had loved his mother. He also thought about how white men had taken advantage of the tribe's weakened state to kill the men and rape the women. He spat at the thought and tried to drive the memory from his head.

Johnny turned to look at their backtrail and shaded his eyes. "Be agittin dark here in a bit. Sun's 'most down. We done lost a whole day by following that crick. We need to find 'em soon Sheriff or we might as well give up on 'em."

They had made it back to the cave, gathered some hardtack, and started again. At one point, they crossed a creek running down the mountainside. Brackett had thought it a separate flow but now realized it to be the same creek. It had doubled back on them. It ran out into the lower sagebrush and offered nothing that could be a hiding place for Nampuh and his bunch. They headed down the waterway until it swung back in a long S turn along the slope to the South. Brackett had been sure Nampuh would come here. The big man would not go near the mines where a couple of hundred hardened miners lived and worked. He now began to wonder if Nampuh might bypass South Mountain and head farther south to Juniper Mountain.

If that were the case, it would be nearly impossible to find them. He slowly shook his head and looked up the draw from which the creek came. The way this water wound back and forth, there could be a dozen nooks and crannies that could hold grass for horses and storage for food and other supplies. Nampuh would have such a cache or maybe several of them. Places he could readily get to and stay out of sight for as long as needed.

The crack of something heavy moving in the willows on the other side of the stream snapped Brackett out of his meditative state. Without thinking, he held the gun in his hand, and he squinted in the fading light to see. This time of year, it could be an elk or deer. He doubted it would be a bear even though this side of the mountain looked like bear country. As a youth, he had once seen a bear, but they were now nearly gone from these mountains. He couldn't see the creek itself, hidden by thick willows on both sides. He again heard the snapping of the dry branches and then the footfalls in the water. He backed away three steps and looked back to Johnny, who watched intently from forty feet upstream. Johnny had his rifle raised halfway to his shoulder as he waited. Brackett motioned for him to back off farther, and he did.

The willows parted, and Plato hopped into view. Brackett holstered his pistol and walked up to the horse. It took him only seconds to see Plato had been badly injured. His entire left rump had burned into roasted flesh. He had several other injuries, as well.

Brackett talked to him quietly for a minute while stroking his neck and then took out his gun. Then, reconsidering, he closely examined the wounds. The magnificent animal might heal with time and care if he could get the horse back to Silver City. Certainly worth a try.

He took off what remained of the hobble ropes. With Johnny's help, they quickly cleared willows on the creek's near side, forming a small corral of sorts. Roughly weaving small willow stems, they made two green ropes to create a weak fence. Brackett knew Plato would recognize the restraint and, unless attacked by a cougar, would stay put.

Within half an hour, they had pulled and cut enough grass to feed the animal, if indeed it would eat, for two or three days. Since the little corral encompassed the creek, water would be plentiful—even enough room for the horse to soak the wounds if it wanted.

CHAPTER THIRTEEN

Amos Kincaid had just started a fire for coffee outside his tent. He spent the day just as he spent every day for the past two months, working his way around the eastern base of South Mountain with pick and shovel. Amos knew well the only real strikes of gold, and then silver had been made on the west side but couldn't get it out of his head; there would be an equal find on the east side, too. He stepped into his tent to retrieve the bag of coffee. He shook his head when he assessed the small amount remaining.

"Damn!" he said to himself.

He tried to figure how many pots he could make from what remained. Then he would be forced to travel the fifteen miles to South Mountain City for supplies. If he limited himself some, he might get by for another five days.

Again, he muttered, "Damn!"

As he stepped out of his tent with the coffee, he saw the hand wielding the knife. The blade penetrated his heart. He didn't fall back but simply sat down, chin on his chest. In that position, he died within seconds.

Dark Coyote entered the tent and looked for something to wrap around his head to cover his missing eye. He flinched with the intense pain, but Dark Coyote had felt pain through much of his life and knew how to set it aside when needed. He found a bandana and tied it off on the side of his head.

That done, he looked around the tent to see a homemade sagebrush chair beside the prospector's bedroll. Searching through the dead man's belongings, he picked up a frying pan, put some bacon in it, and set it on the fire. His people had been given such cooking utilities before he left the reservation. Dark Coyote felt eaten up with hatred, but it didn't diminish his intelligence. He immediately saw the value of the white man's tools.

When run off from Nampuh's band after being injured by the woman, only his knife went with him. Now, he found himself very well outfitted. In addition to the dead man's tent, food, and bedding, he now had a sturdy packhorse standing ten feet away. A saddle and rigging, stored inside, let him know the horse could be ridden. He had enough food to last many days. He would be able to heal in comfort. He moved slowly, deliberately, for any sudden move sent shock waves of pain through the eye socket and all the way to the back of his head. He had no use for the white man's coffee but nearly everything else he found edible.

He searched through every possible part of the camp's contents and finished disappointed when he found the white man did not possess a gun. With the bacon barely cooked, he took the fork he discovered and put the slab on a tin plate to cool. It had been more than a day since he had eaten, and hunger made him anxious. At least the dead man had chosen a campsite next to a creek, and water would be no concern. So too, everything he would need to make a strong bow and arrows existed near the tent. A grove of aspen offered limbs sufficient for a spear. He would be well-armed by the time he had healed enough to move on. With the bacon cooled, he ate until satisfied. He watched the coals slowly turn white and saw the first star make an appearance.

He made his way into the tent and onto the bedroll, where he closed his remaining eye and drifted off to sleep. The body of Amos Kincaid still sat just outside the tent flap. It would stay there for the next five days, being steadily picked at by vultures until dragged away by coyotes drawn to the stench.

It had been a troublesome night for Dark Coyote. He could only sleep for short periods before nightmares or pain would jerk him awake. Still, full-on daylight had come before he awoke the last time. He shivered and tried to pull on Amos Kincaid's coat, but it was too small; he put it around his shoulders.

In a dream, he had seen himself creeping up to a sleeping Nampuh and stabbing the giant over and over until he had no life left in him. Then he went to the two women and slowly tortured and killed them. As he got the fire started, he smiled to himself at the vision. His hatred of white people now took its place equally with his hatred of Nampuh.

Nampuh had not put him out because of his eye but instead because of the women. Nampuh said Dark Coyote could not be trusted around them. Dark Coyote chuckled as he dropped another piece of wood on the small flames. He had to admit, Nampuh had been right. He could not be trusted with those white dogs. He would kill the women and even Nampuh himself, given the slightest opportunity. Again, he replayed the dream and resolved to make it a reality. One way or another, he would stock Nampuh and the women and find a way to exact his revenge.

Nampuh arrived well in advance of the rest, but the women and other men finally got there. The rest of the day and night had been non-eventful for the women. When Nampuh came to check on them, Minnie asked if she and her daughter might be allowed to talk to each other without fear of more beatings.

Nampuh said, “Talk all you want. You will not be mistreated anymore as long as you do as you are told and don’t try to escape.”

He then repeated this to all the men in the camp as he turned away. As soon as he moved away from them, Minnie began to reassure Mercy they would be all right.

“But Mama, what will happen to us when we are sold or traded to another bunch of desperados?”

“I don’t know, Mercy, but we don’t need to worry about that now. We just need to do as we are told and wait for an opportunity to run away.”

“Even if we could get away, where would we go. We’ve come so far and so much at night. I don’t know how to get back home, do you?”

That was a question Minnie had long contemplated but had no answer for, she just shook her head, and the two fell to silence for the rest of the night.

CHAPTER FOURTEEN

Johnny made a small fire as the morning light worked its way down the east side of South Mountain. They had taken a few things with them when they left the cave. Mostly a little food, coffee pot, and two cups wrapped in blankets slung over their shoulders and tied with the remains of the dead horses' reins. The guns and ammunition added to the heaviness of the packs.

Coffee and sizzling bacon brought a welcome change from the hardtack of the previous evening. The smell as the coffee boiled offered a blessing to the nostrils. Finally, Johnny took it off the coals, and as the boiling ceased, he added just enough cold water to settle the grounds and poured some into Brackett's waiting cup. Brackett sipped a little to make room for an added shot of bourbon from his flask.

"Sure don't know how ya drink that stuff. I think it would up and kill me dead," said Johnny.

Brackett thought about that. "Probably will. One of these days."

As Johnny settled back against a rock to eat and drink, the reality of their situation began to creep back into his consciousness. "What yuh thinkin' as to what to do next? Keep followin' up and down the creek?"

"I honestly do not know what else to do, Johnny. This country is not as I remembered it. We may not even be following the same creek as I thought it to be. If we do not follow it on down the mountain a ways more, we just will not know."

"Well, I'm with you. What you said about where they might have a hideout makes sense to me. I say we keep on."

The creek continued to weave its way down, and around the mountain's gentle slope, occasionally, it would be reinforced by the flow of a nearby spring. By mid-day, they were well down the hill and had found nothing. They ran across tracks of unshod horses here and there, but none had the tracks of a giant-sized human or in numbers indicating a group of a dozen or more. They were, Brackett knew, simply small hunting parties from some of the lowland tribes trying to get some big game for the coming winter.

They were about to turn back when something caught Brackett's attention. About fifty feet above the creek, on the other side, the ground in a slight clearing among the fir trees looked to be torn up. He pointed it out to Johnny, and he found what he looked for at the clearing. The largest footprints he had ever seen in his life. Just three and then hoofprints covered, and pine needles absorbed the weight, so no more prints were apparent. He motioned for Johnny to join him. As the boy put his boots back on after wading the creek, his excitement grew steadily.

"How long ago ya reckon?"

"Sometime yesterday. We will see where the hoofprints lead."

"Ya thinkin' the big Indian was with them or following them?"

"In front. The hoofprints covered most of his tracks."

"They are not following the creek," Brackett confirmed after a while.

He pointed up the slope ahead, and it became apparent the tracks began a steeper ascent. Brackett stopped to examine the trail and turned to Johnny.

"Not surprising, but some of these are shod. This one is confusing, though. It looks to be a workhorse. Makes no sense."

Johnny stepped up to take a look.

"I know that horse! That's Old Mike! See how that one print don't have no shoe? He's got'im a broken hoof on his left front, and there ain't nothin' to nail to. So's he just has three shoes. That one ol' hoof is so tough he don't miss it none. That's gotta mean that Mama and Sis are ridin' him, or they wouldn't bother with him. Ya thinkin' that be right?"

"Makes sense. I do not believe they would keep an old workhorse without good reason. Let us see where the trail takes us."

They followed another hour as the trail moved to steeper slopes. Suddenly, the tracks broke away from the route they had followed and turned along an aspen copse and then beneath a rimrock. A narrow animal trail broke through the scree that had flaked off the upper rimrock, making it passable for horses. Periodically, Brackett could see where one of the horses lost its footing and kicked loose shale on the underside of the path before regaining its pace.

"That would be Old Mike," said Johnny, "the good Lord never made a clumsier animal."

Three more hours, and they came across a spring surrounded by grass. A fifty-foot indentation in the side of a great granite wall offered a perfect place for refuge for men and horses alike. At the back of the opening, the remains of several campfires were evident.

Brackett surveyed the area, "This is where they spent last night."

Johnny stood looking intently at something outside the opening and didn't respond. Brackett heard him curse but didn't catch what he said.

"What have you found over there?"

"Blood! And lots of it! Take a look, Sheriff."

Brackett looked over what Johnny examined. Indeed a lot of blood. More than just a cut finger.

"Well, no need to play too much into it, boy. It does not mean it came from your mother or sister. Could be from an animal they cut up."

Johnny looked around and again began searching for the trail the group took that morning. He found it and followed for about fifty feet before returning. Relief showing on his face.

"Old Mike's tracks are still agoin' on up the trail. That must mean that Mama and Sis are still alive."

The trail got more complex with every hundred feet of progress. It became apparent the band dismounted and led the horses up the steeper parts of the track. At one point, the scree gave way to a bit of dirt and widened. Johnny let out a hoot as he noticed two small footprints.

"Those there would be Mama's and Sis's! Way too small for none uh them no-goods!"

The tracks were plain and easy to follow. Nampuh did not attempt to cover his trail. Halfway up the mountainside, a well-developed elk and deer trail headed in a generally south direction horizontally. For at least the time being, the steep climbing had leveled out. Brackett took time to get his wind, study the signs and wait for a lagging Johnny to catch up. Huffing and puffing, Johnny sat down on the trail.

"What do ya make of it?"

"We are falling further behind."

"It's me. My feet hurt so terrible I just can't hardly walk. What are ya thinkin'?"

"Well, we can keep on following to see where this trail takes us. If they are mounted again, they will keep increasing their lead. Given the direction, they may not be stopping on South Mountain at all."

They had traversed the mountainside with the trail working its way up and down through dozens of gulches. With every mile, Brackett knew they were losing ground to the outlaws. Morning turned to mid-afternoon, and the sun hid behind thunderheads rolling in from the South. They were now on the back side of the mountain, and in the distance, the massive Juniper Mountain loomed. Seventeen miles long, thirteen miles wide, with elevations reaching seven or eight thousand feet. Two hundred and twenty square miles of pure ruggedness.

Brackett knew that only the roughest of men, those not wanting to be found, made their way there. A place where good men did not trod. To encounter another man would most likely mean a battle. Even the outcast and outlaws didn't respect the rights of others to be there. Even if of the same mold.

Brackett continued to follow the trail until it told him he now knew precisely where Nampuh and his bunch were taking the women. He stopped and waited for Johnny to catch up.

"They've left the mountain, huh, Sheriff?"

"I believe they have. The trail shows that they are headed for that big range in the distance there."

"How long ya reckon it'll take us to get there?"

"Maybe tomorrow night if we hustle it. Johnny, that's rough territory over there, and we have no supplies. We need to go over to South Mountain City and get horses and supplies."

"But by then." His words drifted off.

"I see no way around it. It could take us a week or more to track them down over there if we can catch them at all."

"I can't give up on them, Sherriff. I'd rather see them dead than living with them animals. I've heard the stories. I know they won't never be the same, but I gotta know they ain't gonna be used by them savages any longer than need be."

"I am not giving up on them, Johnny. Just the opposite. I want to give us the best chance of getting them back."

"Get them back? They probably ain't even my mother and sister no more. Like I said, I done heard them stories. No sir, I just can't leave them to live like that."

"Johnny, you need not think like that. Many women have come back no worse for the experience. Do not give up on them yet."

He turned and took the first step toward South Mountain City.

CHAPTER FIFTEEN

It took the better part of two days in South Mountain City before Brackett could secure the two horses and a mule. It had taken longer than he expected to get to the bustling little town because the work boots Johnny wore had created such rawness he could only hobble along. Brackett had gathered some cottonwood oil from the few trees they found at the bottom of a gully to ease the pain, but it had lasted only a short while. Repeatedly, they had to stop and rest the injured feet.

Once in town, they enlisted the help of a Chinese herbalist to help mend the feet. Still, Johnny could barely walk. Without the horses, it would have been necessary for him to abandon the search. All in all, it had been more than four days since leaving the trail. It would take another day to get back to it, too late in the day to depart. By the time they got back, it would be nearly a week.

On their first day there, Brackett asked around and found a man headed to Silver City. The man had agreed to detour to the far side of South Mountain to see if he could locate Plato. He would nurse the horse back to Silver City with him if he could. Brackett wrote a note to Phil.

"The man with this note has taken his time to find Plato. The horse has been injured and needs care. If this man comes without Plato, pay him twenty dollars. If he has Plato with him, pay him one hundred dollars and get Plato up to Jackson to take care of him."

Brackett signed it, and the man left the following day.

During those days, Nampuh and the Dickerson women had reached his destination and were well dug in. The little valley lounged along the east end of Juniper Mountain, offering a fort-like safety, and ended in a canyon with a fifty-foot waterfall cascading to a pool. Both sides were equally high and could be climbed with only great expertise and willingness. The canyon below the pool kept its high, rock walls but widened. The creek still carried a goodly amount of water and grass-lined its shores. The only way into the fortress came from the east end, and Nampuh had posted guards high in the rimrock. From these positions, they had views for three or four miles.

They arrived at the camp to find several women waiting for them. Two were Mexican, and three more were Indian. To Minnie and Mercy, they looked hard and dangerous. The looks given to the new women sent chills up their spines. Again, the Dickerson women were not tied up at night, but when one of the Indian women brought them food, she first spit on each plate and then dropped them on the ground, so some of the food splashed out. Minnie and Mercy jerked back in shock, making the woman laugh. When Mercy didn't immediately pick up her plate, reeling from disgust, another of the Indians came by and picked it up and stood eating its contents in front of them. She licked the plate clean and then tossed it back on the ground. When the woman got back to the other women, she said something, and they all laughed. Minnie tried to use her fingers to remove what spit she could and then shared the remaining contents with her daughter.

Mercy had been barely able to eat anything since their capture and forced herself, at her mother's urging, to gag down just a little of the stew-like slop. When the plates lay empty, the first Indian woman came to pick them up. As she turned to leave, she kicked dirt on the two captives. The other women laughed again. Mercy cursed at them in defiance and then, embarrassed, looked at her mother and covered her mouth. Minnie looked shocked for a moment and then smiled at her daughter and, looking directly at the group of women, called out the same curses.

"We may be captives, and we may need to watch what we do, but we do not have to sit quietly and be insulted by the likes of them!"

Then, with even more attitude, she again shouted out the insults.

Nampuh left the morning before and had not returned. As the evening grew to dusk, he showed up. All the women jumped up and went to him, but only one stood beside him, holding onto his arm. More slowly, the men gathered. The group stood just far enough away, allowing Minnie and Mercy to make out only a word here and there. Nampuh spoke in English with another man interpreting in some Indian dialect.

Suddenly one of the women stepped closer to the giant and starting screaming at him. The words were foreign to the Dickerson women, but obviously, Nampuh understood. She got out only one long sentence before one of the men jumped between her and Nampuh and slapped her first one side of her face and then the other. The blows were severe enough; she would have been knocked from her feet had the man not been holding her up. He gave her a shove away from the gathering and out of sight. The man said something to Nampuh that seemed apologetic and then went after the woman. They heard an agonizing scream a minute later, and the man returned to the back of the gathering.

"Do you think he killed her, Mama?"

"I don't think so, but we should learn from it. We don't talk back to the men and certainly not to that monster."

"Mama, we just have to get away! We must get away! I would rather starve to death or be eaten by wild animals than stay with these demons!"

Minnie could hear hysteria growing in her daughter. She had to control that, or it would undoubtedly get them both killed or worse. She reached over and pulled her daughter to her and held her close until great heaving sobs erupted. The captors were still engaged in what Nampuh had to say and paid no attention to Minnie and her daughter.

"Strength, strength," she whispered to Mercy.

Finally, the sobs subsided, and Mercy sat up straight. She stared into her mother's eyes with a look of determination, or acceptance of their situation, or maybe something else. Most of all, Mercy had a look of resolve and, yes, strength.

The few days since having to abandon the trail of the Nampuh band seemed to Johnny a month. As Brackett led the way to where they left off, he realized he would not find the route on his own. He had been nearly delirious with foot pain on the way to South Mountain City, looking not right, left, front or back but trudging along, head down. He also felt sure if he lost his horse this time and forced to walk, he would probably die. Even with the treatment of the Chinaman, it still hurt to put any weight on the stirrups. Once, the mule he led jerked back and pulled Johnny around in his saddle, causing him to put much of his weight onto his right foot. For just a moment, the world spun in his head. He cussed and grabbed the saddle horn for stability.

Brackett contemplated cutting cross country to pick up the trail farther toward Juniper Mountain but dismissed that idea. Too often, Nampuh did the unexpected.

"No," he thought, "I will just do it the right way."

He did cut off about a mile he knew wouldn't take too long to backtrack if needed, but it worked out fine, and he found the trail without trouble. He pulled up and looked into the distance. It wouldn't seem such a challenge at less than twenty miles to the mountain, but what lay in between made it a huge one. At least a dozen deep breaks with long patches of rimrock would have to be followed to their end before crossing. Some were on deep gulches. Volcanic shale-like rocks could cut a horse's ankles and hooves. Holes hidden in the brush waited for a misstep causing a broken leg. The twenty miles would take an eagle less than an hour to cross but take him and Johnny days. And then what? Then the chase, if you could call it that, would just be starting. He also wondered if Nampuh would stop at all. He walked Southward! The Great Basin? California? Mexico? If California or Mexico, next to no chance of catching up with him existed.

CHAPTER SIXTEEN

The horse for which Brackett had been forced to settle bore no resemblance to Plato. Nor did Johnny's new mount. They were not mountain horses. Both had been part of a pack train and knew only how to plod along at a slow pace, not much better than riding the pack mule following behind. They constantly stumbled when off a well-established trail. Brackett got off and walked much of the time, not trusting the animal to keep his feet. Johnny had no such option given the condition of his own feet. He alternately cussed and took deep breaths as his mount stumbled and recovered time and time again. The pace grew so slow Brackett called the little caravan to a halt and walked back to where Johnny dejectedly watched his approach.

"Face it, Johnny. This is not going to work. If they are still moving, we are just falling farther behind every hour. We have to make a change."

Johnny thought he knew what might be coming.

"You ain't goin' on without me."

"Look, Johnny, they are heading right for the high country, and it is likely snow will be falling up there any time now. If you will not go back and let me move after them, well, we will go back to Silver City, where we can get some decent horses and a more willing mule. I believe they will rest up for a while on the mountain in front of us before moving on. With luck, we can get ourselves better situated and catch them there. We will not need to follow any trails either way, and we can move quickly. You decide. Let me go on alone, or we go back together. Your call."

Johnny looked at Juniper Mountain in the distance and then at the threatening clouds above.

Shaking his head and letting his chin fall some, "I reckon we best get started back then. I ain't got no blanket septin under this nag's saddle, and if it turns any colder, I'll likely die of it."

He turned the horse around and started back. They made it back to the cave where the fire had happened.

By noon the next day, they were back in Silver City. Johnny's feet were getting better but still tender. He went to the general merchandise store and bought some shoes he thought suitable for walking and riding. The Wellington-style boot began to lose favor among the young men driving herds of cattle from Texas because they had little need for a boot that doubled as a walking shoe. They spent almost all of their time sleeping, eating, or riding. But for Johnny, the Wellington would be perfect. Britain's first Duke of Wellington originally designed the boot type. Johnny had no money, but he now owned the family's mill and the property upon which it set. He used the property as collateral at the store for credit.

Brackett went to Jackson's stable to see if the man he paid had made it back with Plato. He had. Jackson thought the horse probably not as bad off as figured and, given time, might be nearly as good as new. Brackett spent a few minutes talking and stroking Plato before buying two replacement mounts Jackson said were sure-footed mountain horses.

"You want a better mule?"

"No, that was my plan, but there just is not time to mess with one from here on. We need to cover some ground."

Jackson said he would get what he could for the two pack horses and the mule.

"Keep whatever you can get for them. Just take care of Plato for me."

"Don't worry none 'bout Plato. I'll treat him like he's one uh my very own youngins."

"Well, hell, Jackson, I was hoping for a lot better treatment than that."

Jackson chuckled and nodded.

Brackett met with Phil to catch up with what had been happening in his absence. Phil had not gotten much rest. The day after Brackett and Johnny left, two competing mines on War Eagle Mountain had gone to war.

Their two shafts of rich ore had broken through, one to the other. After arguments and threats, shots had suddenly been fired within the tunnels resulting in the death of two owners. The sides quickly brought in professional shooters. Try as he might, Phil had no success in calming the situation.

The town council had sent word to the Governor, who responded quickly with Fort Boise troops. They had arrived just the day before and squelched the warring parties. Legal actions were underway to resolve the issue of ownership. Just when things seemed under control, shots were fired on the steps of the Idaho Hotel just that morning. One of the surviving mine owners had happened upon men loyal to the other company. An argument ensued. Suddenly a gun came into play with one man shot and dying in the street, while the other contender lay in the doctor's office with his life on the line.

On top of that, Phil spent so much time trying to deal with all of the drama; he felt compelled to leave his position as bartender to devote his full attention to the troubles at hand.

"Sounds like you have gotten a lot of everything but sleep. I hope you are not missed too much at the saloon. I will make it right with you for the dollars you have lost," Brackett offered.

"Don't worry about it. I don't spend much, and I'm pretty well off, considering. Honestly, I'm kinda likin' some time away from the place."

"Anything else exciting happened?"

"Well, now that you ask. Would it be illegal if I strung up that bunch of kids that run around here all the time?"

Brackett laughed, "They been up to more shenanigans?"

"Yep. Went down to China Town, climbed up on Chung Sing's roof, and dropped rocks down his chimney. Clogged it up, scared the old fella half to death, and smoked him out. He came runnin' out with a meat cleaver uh kai-yai'n at the top of his lungs. I think he woulda cut them boy's heads off had he caught up with 'em."

Brackett laughed again, which caused him to start coughing, which caused his head to swirl. Phil waited for the coughing to subside.

"You all right, Clay?"

"Oh, yeah. I am fine. Well, welcome to the world of hardnosed sheriffing. Those boys are a handful, all right. You do anything about it."

"Naw, that was just yesterday. Too much other goin' on to mess with 'em. I'll talk to the Townsend boy's old man, and he'll get the word to the other father's, and they will give the kids another whoopin', and they'll stay outta trouble for about a week, and by that time, you should be back to handle it."

"Well, I do not know how I can wait?"

The two men sat at a table just under the stairway going upstairs from the bar to the Idaho Hotel rooms. So involved in the discussion, they had not noticed the three men approaching them: the mayor and two council members.

The mayor led off with a tip of his hat and, "Clay. Phil. We heard you were back in town, Clay, and wanted to talk with both of you."

"Well, here we are, Mayor. Pull up some chairs if you wish."

"Thank you, Clay. We'll do just that."

He motioned to the other two men who followed suit. Settled in, the Mayor started again.

"Clay, you know we've had a hard time defending some of your methods in keeping the town safe."

One of the other men started to interject something and the mayor waived him off.

"Now, when you first got to town," the mayor continued, "I was the one who practically begged you to take the job, and I've tried to convince these newcomers to understand what the town was like back then. I know I made the right decision."

The one who tried to speak before jumped in, "Now, that might well be the truth, but that was back then, and this town ain't like that no more."

Phil couldn't contain his disdain, "Excuse me, Mr. Councilman, have you been in town the last ten days? You do know we had another killing just this morning? One of our most prominent men!"

The councilman folded his arms in front of him and leaned back in his chair. "I know this," he said. "Our women think this man is violent and has little regard for life in general, and they want him gone."

With this, the mayor spoke up again. "Now, with all respect Councilman, the women don't make the decisions in this town. And either do you. Not alone anyhow."

Taking a deep breath, the mayor turned back to Brackett, "Now here's the thing, I've heard from many folks that think you should have been here during all this skirmish up on the mountain and should have handled it. Personally, I think Phil did all that could be done. I don't think anybody says different. It was just that they think you should have been here. Now, here's the problem, Clay; there's word on the street that you are planning on going out again to look for those two women and might be gone again for quite some time. Is that the case?"

"That is the case, Mayor. I will be leaving within the hour."

"Well, that's what we heard. It's just not fair to leave just one man to handle a town like this alone. So, we got us an election coming up in two months, and I think that will take care of things the way it should. But, Clay, you can't be goin' off half-cocked chasing after these women. Remember, your jurisdiction is Silver City and immediate area. Not thirty miles, or who knows how far off. So, here's your orders from your employers, stay put and let the army go after them women."

Taking another deep breath, he leaned back in his chair, waiting for a response from Brackett.

Brackett nodded his understanding to the mayor and then turned to look directly at the two councilmen, "Well, Employers, I agree that one man should not be saddled with taking care of a town like this. I also agree that chasing down Nampuh and those women might be considered outside my jurisdiction. However, those ladies have been residents within my jurisdiction. They were taken from within my jurisdiction. I cannot help but wonder what the feeling would be if they were the family of one of you fine gentlemen."

He didn't wait for an answer. When one of them started to respond, he raised his hand to continue.

"But I will admit, again, the town should not be left without its sheriff for long periods of time. Let me ask you this, can I have fifteen minutes to think this over?"

"Well, of course, Clay," said the mayor.

"Thank you, gentlemen. Phil, would you mind taking a short walk with me?"

Phil nodded and stood up. They walked out the front door of the saloon-side of the hotel and down the boardwalk.

"Phil, you need to be dead honest with me. If I were to decide not to continue as sheriff, would you consider running for the office?"

Phil's head popped up to look directly at his friend. He stopped to face him. For a long moment, he just stared at Brackett before forming an answer.

"When I got out of the war, I swore to myself I would never raise a hand against another fellow countryman again. I guess maybe that all changed when I saw that hombre gettin' ready to back-shoot ya'll that day."

"I will never forget that you saved my life back then," Brackett injected.

Phil shook his head. "I warn't lookin' for no thanks. I just want for ya'll to know what I be thinkin'. "

Brackett nodded his understanding.

"Now, when I agreed to be your deputy, it was just to help out my friend. But now, I guess I am kinda fed up with the bar keeping and maybe thinkin' about looking into some other line of work. Fact is, I been kinda thinkin' I might talk to you about me movin' on to greener pastures."

Brackett again nodded and waited.

"But I have to admit that I do kinda feel at home behind this badge. I was thinkin' I might go down into the valley and see if I couldn't get a badge down there. I know I'm talkin' a lot, but I am tryin' to get around to answerin' yer question. I guess my answer is maybe."

"Well," Brackett chuckled, "that took long enough to get nowhere. Do you suppose you might give me a little more to go on?"

"All righty then, how about this? I would take the job if offered but not if there is any chance you might want to hold on to it. How's that?"

"That is just what I was hoping you would say. I am tired of having folks looking at me the way they do, and out there these past days has helped me realize I am ready to be done with being a lawman. Now, what say you and me go back there and trade that deputy badge in for this sheriff's badge? And while we are at it, be thinking of who you might want for deputies."

Brackett found it hard to tell if the mayor and council members were relieved or nervous about his leaving Silver City for what might be a permanent absence. Nonetheless, they agreed to swear in Phil on the spot and, at Brackett's demand, pay him ten dollars a month more than what they had been paying his predecessor. They also agreed to two full-time deputies if Phil wanted them.

Brackett went over what few details Phil wasn't quite up on and handed over his set of keys to the jail. The new sheriff of Silver City followed him out the door. Brackett looked at the person sitting on the bench when they walked outside and onto the boardwalk. There sat the old Chief. He was holding a cat.

"Aha, Sheriff, I here with cat I stole. What time food?"

CHAPTER SEVENTEEN

Brackett and the kid rode out of town at sunup the following day. Johnny pulled up the collar of his new coat. Early October in the Owyhees is always unpredictable. One day can be shirtsleeve warm, and the subsequent dawn turn up pure white with six inches of snow. No snow, but a brisk breeze came up from the southwest. The first of its kind for that fall, and they would be riding right into its face.

Their newly acquired horses, a dun for Johnny, a pinto for Brackett, both did well through the sage-covered, rock-strewn terrain. They were sure-footed and eager to step out. The two men were making good time and, late in the day, made camp on a small creek at the base of South Mountain.

The several fires in the canyon hideaway made it easy to see the location of every one of Nampuh's outlaws. The night felt colder than any of the two women had been forced to endure previously. They were given just one woolen blanket, ragged, with numerous holes. They also had the saddle blanket taken from Dark Coyote's horse upon his exile. Minnie had been offered his horse, but the animal proved much too high-strung for the inexperienced riders. They did, however, wisely accept his saddle for the workhorse.

The mother and daughter sat with the two blankets wrapped around them as they huddled together. They learned not to give the Nampuh women cause to harass them but also found that once they knew how Minnie had ripped the eye from Dark Coyote, they maintained a respectful distance. Minnie and Mercy were looked at with a new sign of uneasiness.

Nampuh himself had told them the women of his band had been informed of the eye removal. He smiled and said that knowledge would offer Minnie and the girl some protection if they showed no fear and did not present an attitude of challenge. Doing so would force one of the women to answer to save face with the others—a fine line to walk. At least, the meals were brought to them and placed carefully now without apparent contempt.

Only a rare minute passed when Minnie wasn't thinking about escape: she had run a thousand ideas through her mind, but none were realistic. They all involved a significant lapse in the security Nampuh established. She thought the giant could have been a master military planner had he not chosen this life.

The band had built no hogans or even erected a single tepee. It appeared this to be a temporary location with Nampuh simply resting up for a long journey ahead. Over the days they had been there, several more men and women had joined the group. Also, three more captive women were brought in and kept on the other side of the encampment. Minnie had caught only a glance. Their hands were bound.

Just before dark, two newcomers arrived with a teenage captive. The boy tramped along afoot with his hands tied. One of the men rode a Mexican saddle with a rope tethered to it, the other end around the boy's neck, keeping the lad trotting along to keep up. As they came into camp, the boy tripped and fell hard on his face. With his hands tied behind him, he had no way to break the fall. The rider didn't look back and didn't stop.

Being dragged along, the boy tried to keep his head off the ground and rocks. When the horse stopped, the boy quickly tried to gain his feet to avoid dragging. He needn't have bothered, for he had arrived at his destiny. The rider unwrapped the rope from his saddle horn and tossed it aside.

Nampuh walked to the boy. In a loud voice, he announced, "This boy is one of our captives. He was being fed and cared for. He could have had a good life with his new owners in Nevada, but he chose to escape. Bring the other captives to me."

The other three women were hustled forward, and one of the men came to Minnie and Mercy and motioned for them to go with him. They struggled to their feet, and he led the way to a large circle of others.

It shocked Minnie to see the three new women captives were just girls, perhaps thirteen or fourteen years old. She also noticed there were two more young men captives. They, too were bound. They looked to be in their late teenage years. All the Indian women gathered together, making up more than half the females traveling with the band. They were all grinning and almost dancing from foot to foot as if in anticipation. They held limbs measuring two to four feet long and as big around as a man's thumb. The sticks had not been smoothed. The smaller branches simply broken off, left nasty, sharp stubs protruding along all sides.

For the first time, Minnie had a chance to see what she assumed comprised the entire hodgepodge of Indians, Mexicans, Whites, Blacks, and some she just couldn't identify. She thought one might be Chinese but could not be sure. The Indian women made up the majority, but a diversity of other females also joined them. In all, Nampuh's bunch of misfits seemed to number close to thirty. They were a rough-looking assembly, but obviously, Nampuh had total control over all of them.

Nampuh continued, "Now, watch and learn. This is what happens to those who try to escape."

He stepped back from the boy and nodded to the Indian women. A sudden horrific chorus of screams burst forth from them, and they immediately surrounded the boy and began flogging him with their sticks. As one hit him on the head, two others jabbed him with the ends of the torture sticks, and the rest would beat him about his legs, back, and shoulders. The banshee yelling never subsided as the jabbing and beating went on. The boy screamed as blood seemed to be coming from every part of his body. His face nearly unrecognizable; he collapsed under the endless assault and fell to the dirt. The women suddenly stopped screaming and backed away. Minnie watched in something of a stupor, mesmerized by the savagery.

Mercy had initially covered her eyes, but a man had jerked her hands away and, pulling her ear to his mouth, said, “You must watch, or you will be next.” She watched.

Minnie thought the boy had survived his ordeal and felt horrified to see him dragged up off the ground by two Indian men. They tied him to a tree in a way that kept him standing. The women again attacked, first stripping away all of his clothes so the sticks could inflict even more damage. They resumed their screaming and seemed to increase the enthusiasm with which they beat the kid. Now, the jabs were deeply penetrating the flesh. The boy screamed in agony for a while but finally, mercifully, fell from consciousness. Nampuh stepped to one of the women and grabbed her bloody pole as she drew it back for another swing. The other punishers took note and backed away in silence.

Holding the stick high for all to see, he shouted, “Now, you see the beginning of what happens to a person who tries to escape. Think before you try.”

He waved his arms, indicating everyone should resume what they were doing. But even this wasn’t the end. They untied him from the tree and, still unconscious, hauled the boy away. All through the first hours of the night, tortured screams of agony could be heard. Finally, the night went soundless. The captives did not know, could not have known; the wailings were not from the boy. He had died while still tied to the tree. The cries were those of a nightguard posted on the rimrock and not brought about by torture but rather a hoax orchestrated by Nampuh to enhance the fear planted in the captives' souls.

CHAPTER EIGHTEEN

Johnny could smell the coffee and hear the crackling of the fire and swish of horsetails as they warded off the pesky night flies. At least, he thought, the cold would soon do away with the bugs. He listened for another half minute.

"Well," he considered, "that damned wind of the day before has stopped. That's somethin' anyhow."

He opened his eyes and saw the stars were but a few. Sitting up on his blanket, he stomped his way into the new boots. His still painful feet complained but allowed him to stand on them without making him grunt. He pulled on his coat against the morning dew and donned his hat.

Accepting the cup of steam, he tasted the brew without comment as he warmed himself at the fire.

The first sip burned his tongue, and he fought back the urge to spit it out. The next went down easier.

"How far to the mountain, ya reckon?"

Brackett took another sip from his cup and looked south. He could make out the next ridge against the horizon.

"Over that ridge is a long valley that should give us some good traveling. Beyond that, I cannot say. I have not been there. Unless we run into some bad going, I would guess we may get to the first slope by early afternoon. So far, the trail they have left for us is plain. I hope it will continue to be."

They ate their fill of bacon and biscuits, washed out their tin plates and skillet with sand, and packed up. The sun had just peeked over the eastern mountains as the two mounted, and Brackett led the way toward the next ridge.

Five hours later, having skirted the remains of an ancient lava flow and yet another outcropping covered with mountain mahogany, they were on the beginnings of the upward slopes of Juniper Mountain. They spent another hour trying to cut Nampuh's trail, lost at the lava beds. They rode out, one going West and the other going East. Finally, Johnny found the hoof prints. The band had taken a new direction and were now riding along the base of the mountain range to the southeast.

Another hour and, suddenly, the hoofprints took a hard turn to the right and headed straight up the mountain until it merged with a well-worn path. Now, a new twist. At least a dozen more horses had traveled there. Their hoof prints blotted out most of the original tracks left by Nampuh. Brackett couldn't help but wonder if someone else might be tracking Nampuh and his bunch. After a brief bit of thought, he dismissed the idea knowing the only others to follow Nampuh would be Army from Camp Lion. The tracks he saw were not Army stock. Most likely, more raiders were joining or rejoining the main lot.

Brackett believed these newer tracks were laid down at different times. It looked as if they came along in twos or threes but not all at once. The most recent, perhaps just the day before. Then something curious. Mixed in with the hoof prints were the prints of a man! Not large but barefoot. Brackett climbed down from his horse for a closer look. Blood showed through the dirt and pebbles. Following the tracks for a short distance showed signs of the barefoot person stumbling and falling and being dragged short distances.

"What do you make of it," asked Johnny.

"A captive. Being dragged when he fell. He probably had his hands tied. No signs that he used them to break his fall or get himself back on his feet."

"A man then?"

"I believe so."

It seemed to Brackett Johnny had lost the sense of urgency of earlier days but not his determination. He looked to be much older than he had just two weeks before. He mainly rode in silence and rarely asked questions. Brackett realized it had been while still in Silver City since he had heard any kind of comment from the kid. He figured Johnny thought his mother and sister were most likely dead and only hoped to retrieve their bodies. He saw no sign the kid sought revenge. That might come later.

He thought back. Had it not been for his need for vengeance, he wouldn't be here now. Had it gained him anything to kill the men who killed his mother and family? He had no answer for that but also had no regrets. Vengeance! It supposedly drove Nampuh to become what he turned out to be. Indeed revenge drove Brackett's boyhood friend, Knife Thrower, to become Dark Coyote and take the path he did. Now, he wondered, would that need for blood take over young Johnny's life? He couldn't blame the kid if it did.

CHAPTER NINETEEN

They were near the part of Owyhee country well known for outlaw hideaways. True, he needed to be on the outlook for Nampuh but thought it entirely possible they might also run crossways of others just as willing to kill them. The breaks had become closer together, deep trenches of rock and sand and granite slides making it more difficult for the horses to keep their footing. The combinations of juniper and the occasional thicket of aspen mixed with willows threw shadows demanding an extra look.

Brackett sensed rather than saw the danger. He pulled his horse to a stop at the dry bottom where once a bit of water had trickled down from spring runoff. He dismounted on the downhill side and appeared to be tightening his cinch as Johnny stopped just below him.

In a quiet voice, Brackett said, "Climb down and check your cinch. Got quite a climb out of here."

Johnny hesitated before doing as told. Realizing something amiss, he turned his horse in the opposite direction, so he stood nearly shoulder to shoulder with Brackett.

"What is it?"

"I do not know for certain. Something up in that thicket caught my eye, but just a flash. Whatever it may be, it does not belong there. Stay on the other side of your horse, and we will walk up to that stack rock."

They had gone no more than ten feet when the arrow glanced off the dun's saddle horn, followed by another narrowly missing Brackett's head.

"Leave the animals and make a run to the rocks!"

Both grabbed their rifles from the scabbards. Johnny climbed for all he was worth and cussed as two more arrows glanced off rocks within a foot of his chest and feet. Making it to the outcropping of boulders, he dove behind one and looked back for Brackett, expecting him to be right behind him.

Instead, he saw Brackett zigzagging his way straight for the scrub from where the arrows had come. An arrow whished by Brackett's right side, catching the sleeve, and he instinctively dodged to the left but stayed on his feet until finding his way behind a stand of thick chaparral. Brackett dropped and crawled its full length of thirty or forty feet. Arrows plowed into the brush where he first entered the cover. Still, having not seen the attackers, he felt reasonably sure there could be no more than three or four. Whisperings came from below, in the Bannack language. Probably a small hunting party running onto an opportunity to gain horses along with the other things contained in the packs. They most likely didn't expect much resistance.

Secured behind the rocks, Brackett could see Johnny. He could make out a bit of movement in the trees by carefully sticking his head up. When Johnny next looked at him, Brackett motioned to the spot and signaled for him to shoot three quick shots into the area. He got into position to sprint and held up three fingers, then two, then one. Johnny let go three quick rounds. Brackett ran to the far side of the trees concealing the ambushers. Taking time to catch his breath, he slowly started moving, inch by inch, silently, into the grove.

Seemingly out of nowhere, a brave with knife drawn, nearly landed atop him. Brackett caught the knife arm and, using his body as leverage, toppled the Indian over and onto the brave's back. Without hesitation, he dropped to the ground while pulling his revolver. As the Bannack tried to regain his footing, the bullet ripped into his chest. An arrow flashed by Brackett's head as he rolled to the left and shot that Indian. He could hear the steps running away from him, and he jumped up to pursue but heard a rifle shot. Walking out of the trees and brush, he saw the man. He had nearly made it to the horses before Johnny put a bullet in him.

Johnny slowly arose from his hiding place and cautiously looked around him.

"Whar's the others?"

"They will not be bothering us. Just a small hunting party."

Once again underway, it became apparent more tracks had joined the first ones, and Brackett felt confident they were getting close. The terrain had begun to yield more and more potential spots looking as if they might afford hiding places on a long-term basis. And yet, the tracks continued. That old feeling of being watched started up his spine, but he neither saw nor heard anything.

With early evening came a flaming arrow streaking across the camp and smashing into a rock just beyond. Nampuh stood up and looked to the far end of the rimrock, where stood the guard. He watched as the guard motioned to the far end of the canyon, where it opened out into a forested area below. Nampuh talked with a couple of his men and then started to lope up the side of the hill.

The lookout pointed far down the slope, beyond a much lower layer of rhyolite outcropping. At nearly half a mile away, the two riders were almost lost in the haze of a windless evening. Being about ready to leave this place and continue south into Nevada, Nampuh sat down to watch the riders' direction. He could tell they were on the same trail from which his band had come. If the riders were lucky, they would keep going south and not turn up the hillside. Duplicating the path taken by his band would, of necessity, lead to their death. Nampuh's attention sharpened as the travelers neared the point of the turnoff. They would live if the two passed on; if the pair turned upward, they would die.

Brackett pulled rein to study the ground. The well-used trail kept meandering off to the south, but the tracks they had been following veered from that path.

The sign began a steep climb toward several layers of rimrock-type outcroppings, one after another, requiring switchback after switchback to ascend. The question was, ascend to what? He could see nothing looking like a place to hold up. And yet, the tracks were obvious. He could see for at least a mile or more in every direction from where he sat his horse. That provided both the good and the bad. It would apply to anyone lurking out of sight, for they, too, could see Johnny and him. In fact, something told him they were being watched this very minute.

"So, are we not following those tracks? They sure did go that way."

"Yes, they did do that. But where do those tracks lead? I feel that we are being watched, and if we start up there, once out of the trees, we will expose ourselves every bit of the way. Nampuh will most certainly have lookouts posted. We have come too far to ride into an ambush."

Johnny nodded.

"What else can we do? I will not go back if'n I can't find my womenfolk."

"We will not go back, Johnny. But I believe it prudent to ride on for now. Once out of sight, we can scout about to find if they went out another way. We can work our way around from above and perhaps get a look at their camp."

"From above? What gits ya tuh thinkin' we can git above 'em?"

Instantly, Brackett's temper flared. Beginning to find ways to catch himself before letting it get out of control, though, he flashed Johnny a stern look, took a deep breath, and answered his question.

"From where we sit, we can see well up the mountain to above any kind of breaks that might offer a hiding place. No, I am quite certain that they are between here and there. With all these broken rocks, there may well be big areas hidden from our sight."

Brackett urged his horse forward, bypassing the tracks. Nampuh relaxed and watched until they were out of sight. Back at the camp, he summoned his two lieutenants and explained what he saw.

Running Dog and Jose' Domingo listened without questioning before speaking. Running Dog thought it would be good to follow them to make sure they were leaving the area. Jose' thought they should take a small party and ensure they would never show up anywhere again.

Nampuh, as always, listened until the two had finished their say.

"You both make good points. For now, we need to be on our way. If we run into them along the way, we will deal with them. Following them for whatever reason would take more time than I am willing to spend. We will pack up our camp and be ready to leave at first light in the morning. I wish to be in Nevada in three days to meet the Mexican slavers. It is there that we will trade the captives for the guns we need."

For the first time, Running Dog and Jose were told why they kept the captives alive. Nampuh rarely told them more than they needed to know for the day to come. They were shocked.

"And these slavers? They will give us guns? We have guns. Do we need more?"

No sooner than the words came out than the look on Nampuh's face made Jose' wish he could reach out and stuff them back in his mouth.

"Of course," he blurted, "no need to explain. If we did not need them, you would not be trading for them. How stupid I am for the asking."

Hoping he had as least partially covered his mistake, Jose' quickly turned to look at something he pretended had caught his keen sense of hearing.

"We had better get the people started," Nampuh said quietly.

Running Dog and Jose' both nodded their understanding and moved away to give the orders. If they disagreed with Nampuh, they tried never to give the slightest hint of it. Jose' knew he just made an error, and it would not be forgotten.

CHAPTER TWENTY

In case Nampuh's goons should follow, Brackett stayed on the trail, now tracked with only those made by deer and elk, for another two hours before feeling secure in turning back to the mountain. They had to cross two ridges and several smaller gullies to gain the main slope. Still, they were not nearly across the mountain as a whole. It measured miles across. In reality, it wasn't just one mountain, but a range of mountains snugged tightly as if God had put his hands on either end and pushed them together. Now they had the appearance of one large mountain from a distance, but their true nature became dizzying once there.

Easy to get turned around on a day heavy with dark clouds and challenging to know which way to travel without the sun. All this country, unknown and new to Brackett, caused him to look back constantly. Not just to make sure they were not openly followed but to make sure he could recognize landmarks if they were to backtrack. Johnny had some of those same instincts from his several years of hunting. Only once had he gotten lost, and he resolved from that time forward to always know which way home. Still, this proved a wonder to him, vast and wild and dangerous.

Known to his family and their few friends as easy-going and playful, Johnny now had none of that left in him. He now had but one thought, find his mother and sister and, one way or another, release them from the hell they most surely were enduring if, indeed, they were still alive.

"I've got a bad feelin' Sheriff. I'm thinkin' we need to hightail it up that mountain and git that looksee."

"All right, Johnny."

A strong north wind suddenly whipped and coursed its way up the slope, blowing away much of the low cloud cover.

Both broke out their heavy canvas dusters and put them over their coats. Johnny pulled his faded red bandana over his nose and tugged his hat tighter. Both men knew the wind clearing the skies presented just a temporary event. The wind being the leading edge of a storm front. At least, it promised a full moon to the southwest. That would give them some light by which to ride after the sun went down.

They worked their way back and forth on the steep climb, trying to cling to the timber when possible and rock outcroppings when no trees were available for cover. Dark covered the mountains when they had gone as far as the fading moonlight would allow. Brackett stopped and stiffly climbed down from the saddle. The little stand of juniper and aspen mix offered a bit of relief from the wind. He looked up to check the stars for direction and instead got hit by a first snowflake. The only stars were off to the Southwest, where the full moon hung, about to drop from view, taking its light with it. Above where he stood, the clouds had moved in. Brackett cursed the weather and tied the pinto's lead rope to a tree.

"We best try to make us some sort of shelter. Looks like we might get some snow with this wind."

Johnny said, "You build a shelter. I'm going to do some scouting downhill toward where you think they might be."

He dismounted, tied off his horse, and pulled the rifle from its scabbard. He looked at Brackett and pointed down the mountain at a forty-five-degree angle from which they had climbed.

"You reckon that be about the right way?"

"That is the way I figure it, Johnny, but I wish you would help me throw up a windbreak, and then I would go with you."

Johnny ignored that and started downhill.

"Damn kid!" said Brackett under his breath.

He used the little remaining moonlight to find branches with which he could construct a lean-to.

By the time the moon had set, he had been able to lay some cross-members between two trees and applied a series of brush and limbs against them, creating a shelter large enough for the two men to at least keep the coming snow and wind at bay. He unsaddled the horses and stored the gear under the canopy. The horses would have to put up with the weather. Mountain stock was used to surviving elements much harsher than the first snow of the season.

Having done what he could, he began looking and listening for some hint of the kid. He had been gone for over half an hour. About ready to go looking for him, Brackett heard a crackling of dry brush off to his left and caught just enough of a glance to recognize the dark silhouette.

"Hey, over here!" Brackett gave in a loud whisper.

The figure stopped and looked around, unsure from where the voice had come.

"Over here."

Johnny located the direction and half stumbled to him.

"Come near to steppin' on 'em!"

"How far?"

Johnny crawled into the lean-to and, finding his saddle blanket, pulled it over him.

"Might be they be a quarter-mile below. They got them fires agoin', but they look to be packed up and ready to move out come mornin'."

"How many?"

"Don't rightly know. Five or six fires. There be a lot of them, though."

"Were you able to see your mother and sister?"

"Naw, couldn't make out no faces. Hell, I could not even see man from woman. But I think they must be there."

"Alright," said Brackett, "We can get some rest for a few hours, and then we will get close enough to see them when daylight allows."

Mother and daughter were now allowed to wander over to the other captives and sit with them for extended periods before eventually being herded back to their own area. Minnie correctly assumed the beating and torture of the young boy sufficed to scare away any thoughts of escape.

They learned what circumstances brought the others into the camp. Two of the young girls were sisters. Thirteen and fifteen years old. The third girl, a family friend, had been staying with them when the raiders came and killed all of the adults. When finished with the carnage, the bandits brought along the girls.

The two boys and their families had been part of a wagon train headed for Oregon. They had been out hunting sage grouse when the outlaws suddenly surrounded them. They each shot at the renegades but missed and were overcome before they could reload their old cap and ball muskets. After being beaten to the ground, the raiders put ropes around their necks and dragged them along. The kids had lived in fear for more than a month, but one of them showed the still very evident rope burns and scars on his neck. The boy tortured and killed for trying to escape had been captured with them. Both seemed to have given up on any idea of surviving.

Minnie and Mercy did not sleep because of the cold. They had been allowed to sit near the fire in the early night, but when the fire went out and everybody went to their blankets, the two of them were left with nothing more than they had before. The snowflakes fell off and on until just before dawn when it intensified and dropped about an inch of accumulation. They sat shivering, snuggling as they awaited the first signs of the day. The snow continued falling, the darkness lessening as the bit of earthly light reflected on the brilliance of the white rug nature laid before them. Another hour and Minnie peeked from beneath the thin blanket covering their heads. The snow had stopped, and to the east, the slightest hint of light revealed itself on the horizon.

A few dimming stars appeared above as the cloud covering began to recede. The knot in Minnie's stomach returned. The knot, now always a constant companion. The ache not from lack of food, although there was that. No, this ache came not from sickness but rather from her fear. Fear for her daughter, the gut-wrenching loss of her sons, the loss of her husband, the husband she hadn't thought she cared for anymore but now, strangely, missed horribly—the ache from the loss of a life she never had but had dreamed of having. An inside ripping of such intensity, at times, it nearly bent her over with its anger. A burning fire within, searing away her innards, trying to cut to the outside.

Someone tried starting a fire using two stones for sparks. With the scant layer of snow on the ground as a buffer, the repeated clicking of the rocks seemed to be the only sign of life. All else rested in an uneasy silence. Every night of their captivity, they were aware of their captor's presence with the pharyngeal snoring from various parties. Now, even that reminder had fallen still. Eventually, the fire maker gave up and retreated to their blankets.

This time of day, the time Minnie hated most. The hours before daylight when partially awake, the blackness offered nothing more than dread of what might come, the horrific memories of the butchery of her husband and sons, or, worse, to drift off to a restless sleep inflicting hellacious nightdreams. From those nightmares, she would often be shocked awake, ready to do battle with the demons of her mind, only to find herself standing full up with an alarmed Mercy trying to soothe her and urging her to sit back down.

She knew Mercy at least slept some. She could hear her breathing, even and, for the moment, unencumbered. Mercy finally stopped the violent shivering with the wind gone and the snow having stopped. The wet blanket over them had kept them primarily dry beneath.

The clicking of the stones returned. Evidently, the fire starter had rounded up some dry grass or pine needles and was back at it. Then, a tiny light appeared from the sound direction—just a glimmer at first but persistent in its desire to grow. As small bits of fuel were added, the spark learned to crawl, walk, and finally run. Flames rose to a foot high.

Across the way, Minnie could make out the Indian woman who had grown the blaze. The one who had contemptuously tossed the plates of food at their feet on the first night in camp. Since then, she had shown a deal of deference, if not acceptance.

Minnie pulled the blanket back farther so she could look at the sky, and when she glanced beside her, she saw her daughter's eyes were now open wide, and the glow of the fire danced within them.

"How long until they head on out, Mama?"

"Not until first light, but maybe even later if they do not want to deal with the snow. We must wait and see."

"Mama? I had a dream that Daddy sneaked into this camp and rescued us. Do you think somebody might come for us?"

"I don't know. I don't even know if anybody knows we were attacked. We often went for weeks without seeing anybody lest we went to town."

Around the fire, two more figures now huddled. All were women. To the side, out of the firelight, Minnie could hear the familiar sound of flatbread being worked. Judging by the brightness of the stars, daylight would wait at least another hour. She stood up and slowly stretched out her stiff muscles before stepping behind a tree to relieve herself. When she came back, one of the women had walked closer to make sure of her return. Satisfied, the woman hurried back to the warmth of the fire.

Someplace on the other side of the camp, trees began reflecting light as another fire got underway and then another. Soft voices mixed with the crackling of the fires, and men coughed away the morning tobacco congestion. Nampuh appeared at the first fire and said something unintelligible to one woman. He motioned toward Minnie and Mercy, and the woman nodded. She went away from her fire and, in a bit, came carrying firewood and dry pine needles. She said something to

Minnie and Mercy, but they could not understand her language.

Clearing away a circle of snow with her bare hands, the woman crouched between them and the existing fire, blocking the light. She went back to the fire and pulled out a twig with bright coals, brought it back, touched it to the sticks she stacked in the little clearing, and a flame caught. Soon they were being warmed by a small fire.

"Thank you," said Minnie to the woman.

The woman looked at her blankly and went away.

Minnie and Mercy stood near the fire and held their wet blanket over the flames, hoping to dry it out before the breaking of camp. They would need it for warmth once taken away from the fire. The thick tree by which they had been kept for the last week or more, they had both lost track of how many days, had an abundance of dead, dry limbs beneath. They continued to feed the fire from that source and kept it going strong.

By the time the stars fled the horizon and even the distant mountains were in full view, the blanket had dried enough they could fold it up for travel. They hadn't seen Nampuh for quite some time, but his two lieutenants were busy giving orders in preparation for departure. Several of the men cussed back at them but still followed their instructions.

CHAPTER TWENTY ONE

As soon as Brackett and Johnny came out of the lean-to and shaken out their blankets, they saw the dawn would be upon them within minutes. Both had been so exhausted from the strenuous travel of the past days; they slept later than planned. Now, they hurried to find their way through the white cover to where Johnny had spied on Nampuh's outfit the night before. At the halfway point, they smelled the smoke of the fires. They saw the whole bunch, awake and preparing to break camp at the overlook.

Huddled behind the highest points of a rimrock, the two could do nothing but wait. Any opportunity to sneak into the camp and extract the women had been squandered by their late arrival.

"All we can do now is keep out of sight and follow them. Hopefully, your mother and sister are still with them."

Less than an hour later, with the sun breaking over the horizon, two men began to shout orders at the group as a whole. Belongings, on horses and travois, the band started to move down the slope.

"There they are!" exclaimed Johnny in a hushed voice. "The two on the big workhorse just ahead of that last rider."

Brackett nodded, "Their hands are free, and they are not tethered. That means Nampuh is not worried about them escaping or being rescued. That might just give us the chance we need."

Back at their horses, they worked their way along the tree line. Brackett held up his hand to stop their progress. At the bottom, on the trail they had been following, a single figure walked along at a fast pace.

"Nampuh!" said Brackett. "We should wait and see how far back the rest are."

Then, not too far above Nampuh on the opposite hillside but above a rimrock and out of Nampuh's vision, a lone rider came into view, pacing him.

"We have company," said Brackett.

He pointed to the horseman.

"Who do ya think?"

"Do not know. But we best sit tight. If we can see him, then he might see us. He does not seem to be as interested in the main band as he is in Nampuh. I doubt he will be looking our direction, but we will just stay put for a bit."

Nampuh and the unknown rider were soon out of sight over another string of never-ending ridges. Another twenty minutes and moving much slower than their leader came the first members of the outlaw band. The whole of them was strung out. Johnny could make out his womenfolk, and they were not the only captives. They could make out more women, small, probably young girls and at least two men. Those were afoot and stumbled along. Looking closer, Bracket could see the young men had ropes around their necks, tethered to a horse ahead of them. None of the captives appeared to have their hands tied. The two girls were separated from Johnny's people by two horses. The boys were several horses ahead of them.

"We need to keep track of where your mother and sister end up when they camp for the night. Might be we can sneak in and retrieve them after dark."

As much as the terrain permitted, they stayed in the trees and always behind the long string of travelers.

"If I were to ride ahead to see where Nampuh is taking this bunch, would you be good to keep an eye on your mother and sister?"

"You bet, I was athinkin' somethin' along that line muhself. We need to know where they be headin'. Might be that ya can figure a way for us tuh set up when the time comes."

With that agreed, Brackett climbed higher into the trees and trotted ahead, keeping out of sight but watching the trail below. It took him two more hours to finally spot the other rider, still holding his stealth so Nampuh wouldn't see him. On the other hand, Brackett couldn't see Nampuh. The trail disappeared into a deep cut between two ridges lined with granite sides. It wound in a snake-like fashion obscuring most anything within.

Looking to the other side where the horseman rode, Brackett saw he, too, had stopped. The other rider just sat his horse for several minutes and looked into the curving trench below. Eventually, he turned his horse at an angle up the hillside. Brackett watched him out of sight as he topped the ridge.

"Going to get ahead and wait for him," he said to himself, "Not a bad idea."

He started to climb higher on his hillside when he heard a distant, single shot back from where he had come.

"Damn!" he said.

He contemplated what to do before turning back toward Johnny.

Johnny saw the tree limb disintegrate before he heard the report of the shot. He quickly moved farther back and out of sight, urging his horse through the trees and around the end of a rimrock.

He rode as hard as the rocky, uneven ground would allow and cussed himself with every foot gained. Why did he get so close they saw him? He felt the fool. Now, if they caught him, he would not be able to do what he had come to do. Who could know what that might mean for his mother and sister?

He had no doubt some of them would be after him. If they sent trackers after him, he would have no chance. He had heard how relentless Indian trackers could be.

Just as he topped a ridge and hoped to make the other side, another bullet grazed his shoulder, ripping the coat but not hitting the flesh beneath. Then another fractured a rock next to his horse's front hoof making the animal shy to the left, nearly unseating him.

Hanging precariously to one side and trying to regain his saddle, yet another bullet split the air where he would have been sitting. He recovered his seating as the horse plunged down the other side of the small ridge, out of sight of his pursuers. He guided his spooked horse down the draw and toward what he hoped would be a path to Brackett. He didn't think it through. Now, just panic and fear drove him towards the only salvation of which he knew.

No more shots were fired, and after five minutes of running, he pulled rein to look behind him. He saw no riders and slowed to a trot. The fact the heaving horse hadn't injured itself over the rock and hole-infested backtrail appeared a miracle. Johnny began to catch his breath and gather his composure. He rode on without giving any more thought to keep an eye on the procession that kept his abducted mother and sister. Now, he thought only of finding Brackett and being safe.

A half-hour passed without incident when his horse fell from beneath him. He never heard the shot, and at first thought, the horse had stepped into a hole or some such. Then he saw the gaping hole in the neck of the mount, and he knew.

Luck had been with him. The horse had simply collapsed without falling immediately to one side or the other, so he wasn't pinned under it. He jumped first beside it for cover and, with wild eyes, surveyed the hillside behind him for some sight of his chasers. At first, he saw nothing. Then the sun sent off a flash from something metal, a good five hundred yards away. A chill shot up Johnny's spine. He had heard of long guns known to shoot from such a distance but had never seen one.

He grabbed his rifle from the dead horse, took a deep breath, and scrambled farther down the gully to several boulders as high and wide as an elk. Just as he made it to the nearest one, the top of it exploded like it had been dynamited. Splinters of it peppered the side of his face like shotgun pellets. He dove headlong behind it and sat shaking. Never had he felt such overwhelming fear. He knew he couldn't begin to reach the man or men shooting at him with his gun. They would undoubtedly just track him if he tried to run afoot until he became an easy target for that long gun. If he stayed put, he reasoned, they would just work their way around him until they had the shot they wanted. He wanted to, needed to, look over the rock to see if they were coming for him. He willed himself to move, but frozen with fear, could not.

Clouds moved lazily across the blue above, and the bright light came and went in accordance. A breeze grew up, sending dust into his eyes, and then calmed to nothing. The minutes went by, and still, he did not look above the rock for the ones trying to kill him. Might be, he thought, they have given up knowing they had killed his horse, and a man without a horse could not offer much of a danger to a large group of mounted men.

He had almost gathered enough nerve to stand and look when two quick shots rang out from a large patch of chaparral behind him. He heard the bullets whiz by, well over his head and even over the rock. The shots had been from close by and confused him as to why he hadn't been hit. Whirling around and bringing up his pistol, he saw a man running and dodging straight for him. He almost fired when he realized he was looking at Brackett.

"Hold up, Johnny!" Brackett slid in beside him. "What the hell is wrong with you? Why are you not shooting at them?"

"Are they close?" a pale-faced Johnny asked.

"They were! Another hundred feet, they would have been on top of you. They have scrambled back to cover in some rimrock. They are still only about a hundred or so yards up the draw. What happened to your horse?"

"They done shot it. Must have one uh them there long guns."

He pulled himself to his feet and peeked around the side of the rock.

"They were up there in them trees when they shot it out from under me! Damn near got me as I ran here behind this here rock."

"If they were that far away, why did you let them get so close?"

"Guess I was too afeared to take a look. Guess I was just hopin' that since they kilt muh horse, they would jist natural go on their way."

"Well, all right, we need to get out of here. You think you can run back through that bunch of brush that I came from? Your face is pretty bloodied up; you make it?"

"Face is all right, not knowin' it was bleedin'. I can make it."

"Good, gather up your goods, and we will make our break on the count of three."

"I'm ready. I'll do the weavin' like yuh did acomin'."

Johnny took off at the count of three, and Brackett fired two quick shots over the rock in the general direction of their pursuers before following after the kid.

Lead bounced and glanced around them as they ran, but in seconds, they were lost to sight within the chapparal stand. Beyond the chapparal, the ground dropped away into another gulley, and Brackett's horse stood waiting by a small stream.

"Climb up behind me."

"I got too close, and they seen me."

"Thought I told you to stay back out of sight."

"I knowd it, and I knowd I done got us into a heap uh trouble. Where we headed now?"

Brackett just shook his head. They trotted along, and then Brackett turned back up another gulch.

"Best we can do is try to get to some high ground."

They traveled another mile, weaving back and forth up gullies and over ridges, always working to the south. The going grew rough on the horse, carrying two men. They stopped often and dismounted to let the animal catch its breath but kept to a slow trot while mounted. Brackett took time to look for any sign of the three men each time they stopped.

While stopped among an outcropping of granite, a bullet struck next to his foot. He dropped like a rock to the ground and felt lucky he fell behind one of the boulders. The horse bolted away up the sidehill trail they had been following. Brackett looked for Johnny only to be shocked to see him still standing. He reached up and dragged him to the ground as he felt the concussion of the next shot pass his temple.

"What the hell is wrong with you, Boy. You trying to get yourself killed?"

Johnny just looked at him as if to say, "what's the use?"

"Get that rifle up and help me!"

Johnny seemed to come around some and lifted his rifle. Brackett hazarded a look over the rock to be greeted with an instant rifle report. The bullet zoomed over his head, but he had time to locate its origin. He could see all three men below, where they were well engulfed in trees and boulders.

"Damn! They are set. We will be forced to make quick shots and try to move to better ground."

"Just how we gonna git that done?" said Johnny skeptically.

"Well, I am going to lay down a rapid line of fire to keep their heads down, and you are going to run like a cat with its tail on fire over to that rock up the hill. Do not stumble or fall, or you will most likely die. You ready?"

Johnny's eyes told him the fear remained constant.

"Look, we cannot stay here. They will circle us, and we will have no hiding place. They will just pick us off at their will."

Johnny looked at the rock some twenty feet away.

"There's three of 'em! How can I make it? They'll shoot me down like a dog!"

"Could be. There is sure a chance of that. But if you stay here, you will have no chance at all. If you make it, you can lay down fire for me, and I will do the same. If you like, I will go first. Chances are better for the first one because they will not expect it. Your choice. But decide now!"

Johnny gathered himself and said, "On three!"

Brackett shot so quickly with his revolver for the first two-thirds of Johnny's run, that not a shot came his way. The last third told a different story as Brackett emptied the gun, and the three men realized they were out of range for the handgun. Although the shots buzzed all around him, and he stumbled once, Johnny made it to the rock with a finishing dive. After a few seconds of heavy breathing and checking to see if he had been hit, the kid pulled himself to his knees and looked back to Brackett.

Brackett nodded questioningly. Johnny took a deep breath and held up three fingers. He dropped them one at a time and, with the third one, held the rifle up over the rock without looking over it and began firing as fast as he could in the general direction of their antagonists. Brackett jumped up and ran with everything he could muster toward the rock, but the shots Johnny fired did not deter, and return leads glanced off all around the running man until one took his hat off and tugged at his coat shoulder. It had taken less than five seconds, but it seemed like a journey through eternity. He slid in beside Johnny.

"Good job, Johnny!" coughed Brackett as he tried to catch his breath and waited for another gut attack to abate.

"Not so good. You be hit. You're ableedin' from your shoulder."

Brackett didn't realize he had been hit, but now he looked to where Johnny pointed.

"It is not that bad. But I did lose my hat."

He leaned against the rock for half a minute longer before mustering the energy to bend to his side and use the end of his rifle to reach for it, but the hat rested just beyond its length.

He decided if they survived this onslaught, he could retrieve it later. If they did not survive, he wouldn't need it anyway. He turned his attention back to the men below and then to the hillside above, which seemed their only hope for escape.

They were about half the way up a slope adorned with pine trees and volcanic outcroppings, mixed evenly with large, rolling granite faces like the one they huddled behind. A lot of cover for both him and Johnny existed, but it was the space between those brief respites that made for a substantial challenge. Although more open to the renegades' shots from below, the deer and elk trail afforded the best footing. Better might be the pine trees just above them. The tree trunks were ample, but the fallen needles made for slick groundcover on the steep hillside. He took another look below and saw the three had moved apart. They showed a flanking maneuver Brackett knew had to be stopped at all costs.

"We must move on, Johnny! Do you have your wind back yet?"

Johnny looked to be a bit less pale as he nodded.

"All right then, they have split up and have moved apart. They mean to get on both sides of us. If they do, well, that will be that."

"What then? What'll we do?"

"It is a long run up that trail to that next cover, but we might make it because they are on the move, too. Our best bet might be moving straight up behind us to the bigger pine trees where we could climb out of here. Those pine needles will make it hard to keep our footing, though. I will leave it up to you. Try to make the trees above or up the trail in the open. What do you feel best about?"

Before he could answer, a bullet flashed by Brackett's head and into the rock, so close he felt its concussion. He rolled to his side and caught just a glimpse of the assailant, drew his handgun, and fired in one smooth motion. The man let out a yell and fell back.

Brackett had not anticipated they would be foolish enough to get within handgun range, but this one had. He kept his eyes on the tree behind which the man had fallen in case he might get another chance at shooting. Suddenly, the man plunged from behind and tried to run down the hill. He had made only two steps when two more of Brackett's bullets felled him for good.

"Well, that improves the odds some. Now we are even, two of us and two of them."

"I can peek around this here end of this rock to see where the one on this side might be," offered Johnny.

Brackett finished reloading the revolver.

"All right," he said, "I will snap off a couple of quick shots to cover you. Ready?"

Johnny nodded, counted to three aloud. Brackett pumped out three more shots while Johnny leaned around the end of his side. Five seconds later, Johnny pointed at an angle for one and straight down the hill for the other.

"The one down yonder has pulled back a good thirty yards. Must have shaken him some seein' you gun down his buddy. The other one is maybe a hundred yards over that-a-way. He's got his back to us like he might be checking his gun or somethin'."

"Sounds like a good time to make our move. What is it going to be? Pine needles or open trail?"

"I don't like either choice fer sure. Guess we ought to try fer them trees. Looks to me that ifn' we make it, we got a chance at makin' the ridge top."

"I like your logic, Johnny. If we can make the ridge top, we can turn things around and become the hunters instead of the game. On three?"

Johnny swallowed hard and nodded.

"I will keep their heads down, and as soon as you are safe, you do the same for me. I will move when I hear your first shot."

Three fingers, two fingers, one, and Brackett popped up, letting go of three quick shots. Johnny made a go for the first tree but slipped on the pine needle covering, landing flat on his belly. Reaching out, he caught hold of a low-hanging limb and pulled himself on up. He marveled at making it behind the big pine without being shot.

Quickly he began firing at the places where he had seen the two remaining raiders. One shot rang out from the right side but far off target, and Brackett got behind a nearby tree.

From then on, they moved quickly from one tree to another, to another boulder, to more trees, and soon, out of the immediate danger. When Brackett stopped, they had not quite reached the top, and Johnny came gasping for breath beside him.

"Time to put an end to this non-sense, Johnny."

"What's that mean?" Johnny gasped.

"Knowing what I know of that horse I have been riding, he will probably be found just over this ridge munching grass. May be you go find him and wait for me? I will work my way around this knoll and try to do away with those two. If I get lucky, I will get the jump on them."

"Well, just don't go gittin' yersef kilt."

CHAPTER TWENTY TWO

Brackett worked down the draw, and Johnny started up over the small ridge to his left. Johnny took one more look down the slope before dropping over the ridgeline, but Brackett had disappeared. Once again alone, he felt a chill run up his spine. He tightened the grip on his rifle and began his search for the horse.

Brackett had it in his mind the Nampuh men would gather their wits and start a straight-on attempt to overtake him and Johnny. All they had seen of the two men they were chasing had been they were on the run and had little desire to stop and fight unless cornered.

Brackett remembered a rock outcropping where he would be concealed, but just below, through where he and Johnny had made their escape, lay an area of few trees on an otherwise barren slope. He worked his way to the volcanic uprise. Slipping in behind it, he found a natural hole caused by wind and rain, leaving an angled foot-long, six-inch view of the clearing below. He could see all he needed to see without ever looking over the rocks. He leaned his rifle against it and checked the cylinder in his handgun. His stomach, for once, behaved itself, but his head made up for it. He felt a bit dizzy or foggy-headed. The slash in his shoulder made sure he didn't forget it, as well. He did his best to make himself comfortable for the wait.

Brackett didn't need to wait long before he heard distant voices. Then the crunch of a step on a broken branch. With the rifle in his right hand, he watched the trees. Then, he saw the movement fifty yards below and to the left. He eased from side to side of the hole, searching for the other man. Only the one man came into view with no sign of the other. He let the first hombre come far closer than he planned because he didn't know where the other might be lurking. Finally, far to his right, he caught just the slightest hint of movement. By now, the first man stepped cautiously to his left side. If the man looked to his left, he would see him crouching there. Brackett slowly pulled out his handgun and waited for the man to look his way. Not ten feet away. The longer he could wait to shoot this one, the clearer a shot at the one just emerging from the heavier cover.

The man to his left continued stepping uphill, looking every which way except where his prey crouched. Brackett could hardly believe what he saw. The guy just kept creeping up the hillside and never looked down and to his left. As the man gained another ten feet upward, a quick look to his right side let Brackett know the other man came now within fifty feet and without cover.

Brackett laid the handgun on the rock next to him, picked up the rifle, rose at once, and shot the man to his right. Without waiting to see the man fall, he turned to the one up the hill, grasped his handgun, and as the man whirled around, shot him in the midsection. When the man fell, groaning, he walked up to him and looked squarely into his shocked eyes. The man held his stomach, trying to stop the blood flow. He lifted his head an inch to see the man who shot him. He had to look past the barrel of the handgun pointing at his head.

"Some water, señor?"

"What is your name?"

"Juan, Juan Castino." he answered, "Water por favor."

"Why are you hunting us?"

The burning in Juan's gut grew more intense, and he curled up in pain before answering.

"You saw us. You could tell others where we are. Please señor, so dry, water please!"

Brackett said, "You will not need it," and pulled the trigger.

The man shot with the rifle had crawled a couple of yards but sprawled dead by the time Brackett got to him. He walked back down the hillside and found three horses left by the pursuers. The other two he towed along behind him. On the way back, he picked up his hat, brushed it off, and placed it on his head.

He found Johnny waiting with Brackett's horse in the draw, right where he had thought the pinto would be. Johnny's eyes lit up when he recognized him coming over the ridge with two mounts.

"What next?" asked Johnny when close enough to hear.

Brackett climbed down, walked to his gelding, and took the reins from Johnny.

"Look these two over and pick the one you want. We will take the riggings off the other one and let it roam."

Johnny walked around the horses and finally chose the brown.

"I'll take this here one, but I think that's a better saddle, so I'll take that one off the black."

As they began unsaddling the horses, Johnny said, "So, like I done asked before, what's next?"

Brackett propped the unwanted saddle and headstall on the ground under a big juniper tree and covered them with the saddle blanket. Johnny had already cinched up the brown and adjusted the stirrup length.

Brackett walked back to him and said, "As near as I could tell, Nampuh was headed almost due south. I would like to keep an eye on him. It cannot be more than a half-hour ride back to where the rest are treading along. How about I try to catch up with Nampuh, you go back and get an eye on them."

"Where will I be afindin' you?"

"Once you know where they are, just backtrack right through here and keep on due south. Use that far ridge with the nipple on it as a landmark. Once I spot Nampuh and think I have his direction in mind, I will start back to meet up with you. Just stay on that line. We still have a good five hours of light, so that should give us plenty of time."

Johnny nodded and swung into the saddle.

"Oh, and Johnny, if you run across those two bodies, take a look at their guns and see if they are worth packing. Get their ammunition, too."

Johnny nodded again and lightly touched a spur to the brown. The horse gave forth with a slight crow hop, and then the animal obeyed, and they trotted off. Brackett watched them out of sight and then pulled the big pinto around and started in the opposite direction.

CHAPTER TWENTY THREE

Nampuh knew for hours someone followed him, keeping in the trees or back from a rimrock, just out of sight. Once, the man to his left peaked over a rim, and he caught a glance. Another time he saw him move too close to the tree line. And, as much as anything, he felt his presence. The man stayed well out of range of the new repeating rifle Nampuh had secured from a recent raid.

Suddenly, he also felt being watched from the trees above him, on his right. He never saw anything out of the ordinary as he walked along at his fast pace. Still, something told him someone or thing kept the pace up there.

"Gettin' some crowded along here," he mumbled to himself.

He stopped in the curve of a small seasonal creek bed offering protection from any view above. It appeared anybody following him, from right or left, would be forced to either stop and wait or they would come into his sight. He could see for several hundred yards on either side by just raising his head a bit. He studied the area to his right but neither saw nor heard a thing. Turning, he kept a solid vigilance to his left. At length, a horseman crossed from one stand of trees to another. Apparently unaware Nampuh had stopped, the rider felt safe coming out in the open for a brief moment. At that distance, Nampuh couldn't be sure, but just the way the man sat his horse, he thought he might recognize him.

"Ah, is that you, my old friend?" he said aloud.

Having located the follower to his left, he turned back to the right. The feeling just as strong, but he didn't know what stalked from that side, man or beast. Perhaps a cougar? He had more than one encounter over the years with mountain lions. Being afoot, the big cats would follow, waiting for their chance. Few humans roamed this part of the country, and the mountain lions had developed no more fear of men than a deer or an elk. They stalked their prey silently and out of sight until they could find an overhang from which to leap.

Nampuh had the scars on his left shoulder where a big cat had leaped on him and sunk his teeth deep into him before he could grab the thing around the neck and choke the life out of him. The claw marks were probably still over his back as well. No one ever commented on his size or physical characteristics, and he had never asked anyone to look.

The story had been passed along about an early member of his followers who, in anger, had made such a comment. Nampuh had, in blinding speed, reached out and, with one giant hand to his neck, lifted the fool two feet off the ground and crushed his windpipe. He dropped the gasping body to the ground and then stomped the life out of him. After that, nobody dared even look at him in a way suggesting they were appraising his physical size or any other aspect that might be misconstrued.

He chuckled to remember yet another cat encounter. This one simply came walking up the same trail Nampuh followed. Around a bend, and they were face to face just twenty feet apart. The big male most likely had never seen a human before and stopped to assess what stood in front of him. Deciding it might make a good meal, it lowered its head slightly and began a slow advance. When its prey didn't turn to run, he made a bluff charge and then stopped about ten feet away to re-assess. When Nampuh made his own advance, the mountain lion waved its tail slowly from side to side. Never taking his eyes off the cat, Nampuh reached down, picked up a rock as large as his hand, and hurled it into the animal's chest. The cat let out a scream and then turned and ran back down the trail.

Somehow, Nampuh didn't think a mountain lion watched. He didn't know what it might be but certainly felt its presence. When ten minutes passed without seeing or hearing anything else, he looked again to the spot where he saw the man on the horse. Nothing there. He stood up and resumed walking.

Minnie and Mercy watched the three men charge up the hillside. Later they heard many distant shots, and then after much more time, more shots echoed from yet farther away. Then, silence. It didn't seem like the shooters were going after game. There had been plenty of meat brought into the group without going so far away. Also, just a shot or two usually echoed before the hunters returned with an elk or deer. It had been hours since the three men left.

The two leaders of the renegades talked and pointed where the last shots had been fired. They seemed to be disagreeing about what should be done. Finally, one pointed up the trail they had been following, and the other seemed to consent. One of them shouted back at the pack, and they were once again on the way somewhere—a place most likely known only to Nampuh.

Because of the slow pace, Minnie and Mercy often walked to stretch their legs. Nobody seemed to pay any attention to them most of the time. They were only noted when they were given food or got too close to one of the other captives. Even when one of them departed the caravan to relieve themselves, no concern seemed apparent as long as the other stayed in line. The assumption being, one would not leave the other.

Although tired, the captives had no trouble keeping up now as the entire entourage moved forward. The travois could only be pulled along so fast, slower than an unburdened person would normally walk. Even though every gang member had a horse to ride, many others also walked much of the time. For Minnie and Mercy, since one always had to ride behind the saddle, being allowed to walk, most of the time, brought more comfort than the back seat. The day seemed to get colder as it wore on. They kept the blanket wrapped around them in turns. They talked about the coming night, and while the clouds had moved away and there didn't seem much chance of snow or rain, but the clearing sky gave warning, the temperature would drop below freezing, and they couldn't imagine how they were going to stay warm enough. Survival and what would happen to them when they reached Nampuh's destination had become their only concerns and just about their only topic of conversation. Since giving up on escape, little else seemed to be important.

They had no idea how far they had come during the hours since the camp had been broken shortly after daylight. Mercy often rubbed her stomach to ease the pain caused by gut-wrenching fear. She knew Minnie to be truly beautiful, and folks said she favored her mother, so figured she might be pretty, too. What if the two were to be sold separately and would never see each other again? She held her belly again against the agony.

Her dreams at night had been horrible, but now they often haunted her during the day. Minnie could hear her groaning with the knot in her stomach but had no words of reassurance to offer. She knew Mercy's worst fears not only could but most probably would come true. The equally painful knot in her own stomach never stopped. During the last couple of hours, she had begun to think about something unimaginable. She began to wonder if she should somehow take the lives of her daughter and herself. Would it not be better to be dead than be subjected to the life she believed awaited them? She began to think so. But how could she? She tried to put it out of her mind, but it kept creeping back. All of a sudden, she couldn't look at Mercy without cringing. She had a terribly difficult time replying to her questions. Tears streamed down her cheeks with the agony of her thoughts.

"Please, please, Jesus! Take away these thoughts and give me strength. Tell me what to do."

Over and over, she pleaded for the comfort she had always felt when talking with her Savior but found no comfort this time. Though surrounded by her daughter's love and surrounded by all those other people, she felt utterly alone and without hope. Of course, the cold she felt came from the weather, but even more so, from within her very soul. Walking along, she noticed, at first a haze in her vision, and then something like blindness. A dark fog closed in on her. She couldn't see where to step next.

When she awakened, the sun shone low in the western sky, and she could feel arms around her from behind. She blinked several times, and her head began to clear. She looked down at the hands clasped around her waist and knew they belonged to Mercy, and they were holding her upright in the saddle of the workhorse.

"What happened?" she asked in as much of a steady voice as she could muster.

"Oh, Mama, thank God! I've been so worried."

"What happened?"

"You fainted. You fell, and I was afraid they were going to punish you, but they didn't. The two men behind us just got off their horses and picked you up and put you on the horse, and then one of them plopped me up behind you and, and, I was so afraid Mama."

"I am fine now. Don't worry."

The workhorse plodded along—one hard, jostling step after another. The sun continued to sink lower, and the temperature continued to drop.

Johnny found the procession and, after watching them for a few minutes, started back the way he had come. He hadn't stopped to look at the guns of the dead men, but he dismounted and looked them over closely on the way back. Two of the men were Mexican-looking, and the third definitely Indian.

One rifle, a new repeating type, needed cleaning but otherwise in pretty good shape. The handguns were of standard military production. But, there on the ground, next to one of the dead pursuers, the long gun. The weapon appeared used but in perfect condition. Johnny removed the bandolier, sashed around the dead shooter, and put it on. The cartridges were nearly half again as long as his own rifle bullets. He collected all the other guns and ammunition and slung the belts over his saddle horn. The long gun he carried in his right hand.

As he rode away, he looked back after traveling about a hundred yards and saw two vultures at the Indian man's bare chest. A shudder went up his spine; he spit and rode on.

Johnny wanted to catch up with Brackett before nightfall and kept pushing the horse at a smooth trot. It would be an hour, at least, before the sun would settle in the west, and he made good time getting back to the gulch where he had last seen Brackett.

He didn't hesitate and pushed over the next ridge, catching sight of the nipple-like volcanic vent on a far crest, but thought to meet Brackett long before getting there. He wrapped the blanket over the back of his head and ears and around his coat, allowing the rest to cover the upper part of his legs. He reached to the horse's neck and patted it. "Gonna git colder yet, old son." He nudged the flanks with his spurs, and the brown stepped out once more.

Nampuh appeared to have a destination in mind for the night as he marched along. Although Brackett knew he looked to all sides, just as any savvy mountain man would do, he rarely showed a sign of it. Once in a while, Brackett could detect the slightest hint of a head turn, but it didn't occur often. Certainly, Nampuh, like himself, had developed a keen sense of his surroundings and a better than normal peripheral vision. Brackett stayed well back and high up in the trees.

Suddenly! He could not see Nampuh! Brackett looked much farther ahead of where he thought Nampuh could have traveled but saw no sign. The terrain through which the giant treaded offered minimal opportunity to hide. It had opened up into a wide drainage, mostly void of trees and no large rocks or volcanic breaks. The few junipers could only hide animals or humans if they were up in its branches. The trail Nampuh followed went directly through the middle of this basin. Brackett had been watching but knew he must go higher to stay out of sight if the man were to look back suddenly. He had pushed the pinto straight up the hillside to the top of the wooded ridge, not worrying about losing sight of Nampuh in the vast plain below. At his steady pace, it should take him at least half an hour to start up the next angling ridge ahead.

Yet, when Brackett came back to a viewpoint just ten minutes later, nowhere could Nampuh be seen. He looked far to the other side of the basin and scanned the long, gradual slope for some sign of the other rider. At first, only stillness, then movement as a lone figure stepped from behind a juniper. Brackett still couldn't make out the face but could tell the man searched the entire length and width of the basin and appeared as confused as himself. He also had obviously lost contact with Nampuh. After a few more minutes, the man went back behind the juniper and then emerged again on his horse, taking to higher ground at a lope. Once high enough and having gained the protection of more breaks running parallel to the basin, he cut back to the south. Brackett had no way of knowing if the rider had spotted Nampuh and hoped to get ahead of him or if he decided Nampuh must be somewhere beyond and thought to overtake him.

Brackett remounted and traveled through the heavily wooded trees on his ridgeline at a fair pace. He didn't believe Nampuh could have gotten that far ahead, but he needed a different vantage point from which to scan the lowlands for him. When he once again found a point where he could look clearly down on the basin, the sight of a volcanic trench amazed him. The gorge crossed at a forty-five-degree angle. It hadn't been visible before, and Brackett could tell a person would need to be just about where he now stood to see it. Because of the embankments on either side, it just didn't show up unless right in line with it. The gully appeared to run up and down in depth from perhaps ten feet at places to 15 or more feet at others. It wound slightly, snake-like, so portions were out of sight from his angle. He traced the gorge from its beginning across the basin toward him until it disappeared below the hill line upon which he stood. He could tell it continued beneath him, but the trees blocked any hope of seeing it. He felt sure this would be where Nampuh now lurked, watching for anyone who might be following him. He wondered if he, himself, had already been spotted. He looked to the west, over ridge after ridge, where the sun made a steady descent. Taking another search of the ravine, seeing nothing, he decided to head back to meet up with Johnny. Here, Nampuh would spend the night and wait for his tribe to catch up with him in the morning.

He spotted Johnny about a quarter-mile away, topping a ridge just at dusk. He waived, and after several seconds, Johnny saw him and waved back. They found a protected area beneath a series of staggered volcanic overhangs. They chose one out of the light breeze. Hot coffee and for Brackett, his jug of bourbon, topped off a meal of bacon, biscuits, and fried spuds. Johnny pulled out his pipe and leaned back against his saddle.

"You athinkin' that monster will stay put till his people catch up with him in the mornin'?"

"That is what I am guessing, but we will do what we did today and keep track of your mother and sister. I will ride on up to see what I can see of Nampuh while you watch your kinfolk. Once I find Nampuh, I will come back to find you."

"Any idee how we might be gittin my ma and sis away from them savages?"

Brackett considered this as he had been doing all along.

"I believe that if we can stay with them, there will come a time when we can get them away. I cannot tell you when or where, but I do think it will happen."

Johnny nodded, laid his pipe aside, scooted down on the saddle blanket he used as a ground cover, pulled two blankets over his coat shoulders, and closed his eyes. Brackett watched the stars for a while, tried to find a position that didn't further aggravate his injured shoulder, and did the same.

CHAPTER TWENTY FOUR

The stars were fading in the east when Johnny opened his eyes. Brackett stood over the fire tending a boiling pot of leftover coffee. Bacon sizzled in the pan. Tin plates rested on rocks next to the flame, melting the grease left from the previous night's supper.

"Nothin' better'n a good meltin' tuh clean up them plates," Johnny said.

Brackett looked at Johnny in the flickering firelight, "Thought you were still asleep."

"Nope, jist awaitin fer yuh tuh do all the fixin so I wouldn't need to."

Brackett smiled and tossed a cold biscuit to the kid, "Well, you can get up now. All the cooking is done, but you get to pack the horses before we head out."

Johnny heard them before he saw them. The tribe emerged below him, coming out of a stand of cottonwoods lining a dry creek bed. They were still following the path taken by Nampuh. He made sure to keep his distance and stay out of sight this time. He spotted his mother on the workhorse and his sister leading it on foot. There was just enough light, barely daylight, and the eastern sky yellow above the mountains before the sun broke the horizon. In the little valley through which they traveled, he didn't need to see their faces to recognize his sister's stature and way of walking. The big workhorse was equally apparent.

Brackett returned to where he believed Nampuh would be waiting below. As the sun began to break over the eastern edge of the long, sloping hillside opposite him, he thought he could see some movement. He had to shade his eyes as the sun popped up and the lower area remained in shadows. Just emerging from where the gorge began across the way, a man worked his way up the hill. He tackled the slope as if he were walking on flat ground—long strides, without hesitation.

"You know about the man following you. You are going up to find him, are you not?" Brackett spoke to himself just above a whisper.

Then another movement caught his attention much farther up the slope. It appeared to be the mysterious rider returning to the search.

"Ah, good timing, too. He has come back to you," Brackett murmured and settled back behind a sandstone embankment, only his head poking out above to watch the play on the other side. He could see what the two actors in the developing drama could not see. He could see both of them at the same time. The hillside where Nampuh started his ascent appeared relatively gradual, but about a hundred yards or so, a significant basalt ridge rose steeply above him. It gained some fifty feet and then dipped immediately lower ten or more feet before resuming its slow rise toward the long, high ridge.

In that dip, the rider followed back to his present position. He dismounted and walked toward the edge of the basalt ridge but stayed far enough back he could not be seen from below. From there, peeking over the top, he could finally see the volcanic trench where Nampuh had stopped and disappeared. For a long time, the man stood scanning not only the cut across the basin but also both sides.

Below, Brackett watched as Nampuh continued to come ever closer to the base of the steep bank. It would be interesting to see how he planned on scaling it. Then Nampuh stopped and tilted his head a little, obviously listening intently. Suddenly, he bent over in a stalking type of crouch and began trotting along parallel to the ridge.

"You are doing just right. Stay low, so he cannot see you," mused Brackett.

As Nampuh came closer to where the rock wall petered out, he slowed but kept the crouch. Another few yards and he would be able to look back along the top where the rider remounted his horse. That would put them more than a hundred yards apart. Back on his horse, the rider saw Nampuh's movement just as the big man came into view. The rider seemed caught off guard for just a few seconds and then swung his horse away and, digging his heels into its flanks, held on as the animal shot away.

Nampuh didn't take so much as a step toward the horseman but watched the rider out of sight and then started back down the slope. Apparently satisfied, he came about half way back down and then stopped, and Brackett could tell he stood looking right at his part of the mountainside.

Confident he could not be seen from such a distance, never-the-less, Brackett was convinced Nampuh could sense his presence. Another look and Brackett saw the rider making his way back along the ridgetop in the direction of the tribe. It appeared after being discovered; he no longer held an interest in following Nampuh.

As Nampuh disappeared once more into the depths of the ravine, Brackett worked his way back to where he had stashed his horse and started back to find Johnny. Just a hundred yards on, and Johnny came into sight.

"They'll be here in less than an hour," he said as he approached.

"All right, Nampuh is down in the that trench, waiting. That is what we will do. We will wait. If the moon cooperates, we should have our chance tonight."

The band of outcasts with their prisoners plodded along steadily down the center of the expansive space. The trail angled off to the right until it disappeared without warning, and the riders up front began vanishing into the ground. Minnie and Mercy were perplexed until they drew close enough to see the procession working its way down a steep path into a volcanic furrow, unseen until on top of it.

By the time they made it to the bottom, the leaders were off their horses, conversing with Nampuh. Looking around, they saw several caverns in the sides of the trench big enough for half a dozen or more people to be out of the weather and still have a protected fire. Others would hold a couple of people if they crawled inside. Into one of these small holes, Minnie and Mercy were directed. The horse left with them; they followed the lead of the others and took off its saddle and blanket.

A few minutes later, Nampuh walked by them and nodded. Then he came back and squatted down.

"We will stay here for a few days. Gather wood. You will find much scattered the length of this gulley. Do not leave the gulley. Only one of you go at a time to find the wood."

He didn't wait for a reply but continued on his way.

Brackett moved like a ghost through the blackness of night, smelling the lookout and hearing his breathing. No more than five feet away, he knew the man's attention would be directed to the north, for if any threat should exist, it should be coming from that direction. Another step and he could finally make out the form. The lookout sensed a presence and spun around.

Brackett's knife plunged into the man's heart, quickly withdrew, and found its way to the throat. He grabbed around the body and slowly let it to the ground. Searching and feeling, he found a nearby wagon wheel-sized rock. Returning to the body, he pulled it to the rock.

To anyone coming to relieve him, the dead man would look to be sleeping.

The moon gave promise of rising in the eastern sky. Soon it would be up, and there would be enough light to move about. He sat down in a crag some ten feet away and deep enough to hide all but the upper half of his head. He kept his knife in one hand and, with the other, reached beneath his bottom to remove a sharp stone digging into his buttock. Quietly laying the offending stone aside, he massaged his wounded shoulder and settled in to wait.

An hour later, the moon full up, Brackett saw the movement emerging from the rim of the fissure that held Nampuh and his rabble. It would be the replacement guard coming to relieve the one he killed. The new arrival saw the man at the rock and called to him in a hushed voice. Getting no reply, he walked up and kicked the man in the leg. The dead man lopped over to one side. Brackett leaped and stabbed the man from behind. He had intended to get his free hand over the man's mouth to stifle any sound, but he missed his grip, and a loud grunt emitted into the silence of the night.

He quickly dragged the body to the boulder and propped him up. He repositioned the first guard to rest beside the other and returned to his hiding place. Half an hour later, he felt convinced no others had heard the cry. He could continue his task at hand.

As he hoped, Johnny had done just as instructed and waited, out of sight on the other side of the cut, lined up with a turn, around which any of Nampuh's bunch trying to escape would necessarily be forced to take. It would be a slaughter, but with two rifles and two handguns, Johnny should be able to eliminate those who first came into sight. The rest would surely turn back.

"We should wait until first light when we can see, but they will most likely be sleeping in. There had been a lot of drinking going on before things got quiet. Be aware of the captives when you shoot," Brackett urged before they split up.

Johnny had simply nodded and moved away to his position. Brackett crossed to his chosen post, where he could see the sleeping. The campfires were still going, making it easy for him to see every soul below but difficult for any of them, somewhat blinded by the firelight, to see him. On the other side of the cut, he could make out the form of the other lookout. His shot to take out that man would be Johnny's cue to get ready. He settled back down and pulled the collar of his coat farther up his neck. His stomach caused him pain, and he felt like he might have a fever. A chill made him shiver. He felt for his flask, but it was gone.

CHAPTER TWENTY FIVE

The moon had gone down, but the east's sky was heating up. He couldn't see the guard on the other side, but he knew the man waited there.

Two of the camp's women got up and added wood to smoldering coals, igniting flames for cooking. The fires were of some benefit in spotting the sleepers. Still, he would wait for daylight. The eastern sky slowly lit up as a few of the party below began to move around. Primarily women, he thought. As he had anticipated, most of the people were still tucked away in their blankets. With the full light of dawn, a bit before sunrise, he felt eager to get on with the task. He hoped to get as many as he could while they were still in their blankets.

He had raised his rifle when he saw the figure below, moving with stealth through the sleeping forms below. He brought his gun down to watch. The women at the fires were busy making bread. If they saw him, they didn't recognize him.

The man slowly approached a dark spot on a ledge Brackett had not previously noted.

Suddenly, with a mountain lion scream, the slinking figure sprung like a cat, and Brackett saw the flash of a blade. It looked as if the knife must have found its mark, but immediately, the would-be assassin went flying to the gulley floor. The target erupted from his bed and fell upon the other with astounding speed. The identity of the intended victim was immediately evident even in the low light of the early dawn and flickering campfires: Nampuh!

The attacker took a swing with his knife, and the big man aptly stepped aside while reaching out with a massive paw and grasping the other man's knife-hand. Brackett heard the breaking of the assailant's arm and saw the flash of the knife flying off to the side. Instantly, the entire camp came awake, up and watching. Brackett could see a patch over one of the intruder's eyes in the light of a fire. The two men stepped back for a better look at each other, and Nampuh spoke.

"Dark Coyote, you have returned. I saw you following me before. I have been expecting you. I told you that you would die if you came back."

The episode shocked Brackett. Dark Coyote! His childhood friend, Knife Thrower! Without thinking, Brackett began shooting into the men and women as they gathered to watch. He had counted the number of sleeping bodies and had located the captives. Recognizing the big workhorse, he knew precisely where Johnny's mother and sister slept. On both sides of them had been men sleeping uncomfortably close. Brackett had intended to shoot the lookout and then the two men beside the women before opening up randomly on the rest. He had no qualms about shooting males or females. He knew well the women in the group were every bit as deadly as the men and could most likely shoot just as well.

A bullet slammed into the rock beside him. The lookout! He had forgotten. He dove to the ground and sent two quick shots toward the guard. Then he turned back to the scrambling group below. He couldn't see Nampuh, but he saw Knife Thrower trying to make his way up and out of the cut, his broken arm hanging beside him. He would emerge less than ten feet from Brackett if he kept on his route. Bullets were zooming around from below, but they couldn't hit him with his head below the rim. He squirmed around to where he could see the lookout. Gone. He didn't think he hit him, so he would need to keep his eyes open. Looking again to where he last saw Knife Thrower, he got a glimpse of him moving away on a ledge. Then he saw the movement across the way. The lookout lined up a shot at Knife Thrower. Brackett aimed and dropped the man. Knife Thrower gave no acknowledgment and continued on his way. He had rounded enough of a turn in the gulley to be out of sight of the encampment.

Brackett heard shots coming from Johnny's location. Raising enough to look at the scene below, he saw members of the group rushing back around the jog in the gulley, escaping the infliction of Johnny's barrage. Brackett rose once more, exposing only his head and reloaded weapons, and again started unloading on the renegades below. He watched one of the people raise a rifle and shoot some of the captives. Through the black-powder smoke, he could not tell whether man or woman. Brackett shot the person before they could move closer to do the same to Johnny's mother and sister. Three of the men, he felt pretty sure they were men, had rushed over, grabbing the woman and the girl. The women fought back, getting the mother's dress ripped from her shoulders to her waist. The men dragged her behind some rocks and out of his sight. One of the women from the tribe grabbed the girl and hustled her to the far side, keeping her safe from Johnny's bullets. Brackett again aimed and dropped the remaining people within his sight. Slowly, methodically, as the gun smoke cleared, he took count of the bodies. He sat up now, in plain sight but with the rifle at his shoulder. Each time he saw movement, he would lay down a shot, driving the person back into cover. Twice in the following hour, he heard the report of Johnny's gun. The sun rose over the horizon, but clouds muffled its light.

Brackett waited for one more sign of movement to let go another warning shot. He wanted them to know he remained there. His opportunity came when one of the men who dragged away Minnie Dickerson made a run for a fallen rifle just four feet away. Brackett snapped off a pistol shot. The wounded man regained his feet and hurried back to cover without the gun.

Brackett had been waiting for just such an opportunity. Now he felt good about leaving his position and rejoining Johnny to see what he had accomplished. One more thing to do first. He moved along the edge until he located the hidden Indian woman holding onto

Mercy Dickerson. The woman had the girl in front of her, using her as a shield. A portion of her head remained exposed so she could still look about. Brackett took a deep breath, held it, and squeezed the trigger. The blood splattered all over Mercy, and she screamed and rolled into a sobbing ball, not moving as if glued to the sand. There seemed no quick way to get to her, so he hoped she would just stay put. He arose and rejoined Johnny.

"Let us make a count, Johnny."

"I din't let none of 'em git away!" Drawled Johnny.

He didn't look up, his eyes still focused on the men he had killed.

"You did well. There can be only a few left by my count—perhaps three or four. Three of them are holding your mother hostage. I shot one, though, so I am guessing only two are still a threat."

"What 'bout that biggun'? Ya git him?"

"No, he disappeared right after the shooting started. He had no stomach for being a fish in a barrel and obviously no loyalty to his band of cutthroats."

He looked at Johnny for reaction and saw none. The boy seemed void of feeling.

"You stay here and watch. I will see if I can urge the ones with your mother to come around the bluff. If I move a bit higher, I should be able to put a round or two close enough to make them look for better surroundings. If I am right, they will bring your mother with them as a shield. When they do, you take the one on the right, and I will get the other one."

Johnny nodded but said nothing. Brackett worked his way up and across the end of the trench until he could see one man's feet. They were evidently tightly huddled in a slight recess. Farther along, he could see Mercy, still face down in the sand and still sobbing with great heaves. Two shots into the foot of one man brought them hurrying toward Johnny. They dragged Minnie along.

CHAPTER TWENTY SIX

His mother stood there, naked from the waist up, a slash across her face, blood running down her chin, flowing onto her chest and stomach. Two Indians held her, one on each side, keeping her from collapse. Johnny raised the rifle but shook too much to hit anybody. He crept to a higher rock and steadied the gun on it. Taking a deep breath, he slowly pulled the trigger. The impact thrust Minnie Dickerson backward as if jerked by a rope. The shot to her heart hit with such force it tore her from the grasps of the two men. They stood there for a moment in apparent shock.

"Ahm sorry, Mama. There jist warn't no other way."

Johnny rose up and shot the man on the right as a shot from behind dropped the other. Brackett came bounding down the slope, having witnessed what had just happened. He assumed Johnny had mistakenly hit his mother in his haste. But then, looking into Johnny's eyes and hearing his following statement caused him doubt.

"I got tuh be findin' muh sister."

He didn't look at Brackett, and his eyes were an empty glaze. By Brackett's count, there should be just one more of the tribe left. The wounded man who had tried to retrieve the rifle. He took Johnny by the arm and told him to stay put.

"I got tuh be findin' muh sister," he repeated.

"Damnit, Johnny, stay here. I will bring your sister to you."

Brackett climbed down to the sandy floor of the trench and made his way to where the wounded man should be. Before he rounded the turn, he heard a scream. He hurried around, pistol in hand, cocked and ready.

What he saw made him hesitate. There in front of him crouched Knife Thrower, his boyhood friend. He held the wounded Mexican's scalp as the man struggled to get loose. He looked up at Brackett and, as he stood, let go of the hair, and as the man collapsed, Dark Coyote nonchalantly swiped his knife across the Mexican's throat.

"Knife Thrower, I have missed you, my old friend," Brackett said in a calm voice.

His childhood friend turned to face him squarely, and Brackett saw the patch over the eye. Knife Thrower hesitated, taking a moment to realize who he saw in front of him.

"Clay Brackett, I am no longer Knife Thrower. That boy was weak. I am Dark Coyote. I am strong. Dark Coyote has no friends from his childhood. I have heard that Clay Brackett turned into a white man, choosing to live with the white man. Living with the white man that killed my mother and your mother. To me, you are just another white man. I kill every white man that I find, and now, I will kill you."

He put the knife into a fighting position and began to walk forward. Brackett backed up, holding his now empty hands in front of him.

"It is true that I have lived among the whites. But I killed the ones that killed our families. Not all whites are bad. Do not make me fight you, my old friend."

Dark Coyote continued to advance.

"You can fight or not fight; it does not matter. I will kill you either way and add your scalp to my belt."

"You have just one eye, and your arm is broken. I do not think you will kill me. I wish you would not try."

Dark Coyote began running toward Brackett. The talking over, he lunged as he reached Brackett, who barely avoided the knife thrust. Still, he took the bulk of Dark Coyote's charge against his shoulder. He fell onto his back, and before he could recover, Dark Coyote jumped on top of him, knees pinning his arms even as the knife raised to plunge into his chest.

Brackett used all his strength to kick up with his right leg, landing his knee squarely in his old friend's back, knocking him forward. The knife glazed Brackett's already wounded shoulder, drawing more blood, but the move threw Dark Coyote just enough off balance to give Brackett a chance to find purchase. He wrenched his right shoulder loose and slugged the other man in the jaw with a jarring jab. Dark Coyote rolled off but held onto the knife. His broken arm slinking to one side, he again crouched for a charge. They stood ten feet apart, both breathing hard. Brackett's arm now had two wounds in it, and it began to stiffen. He stood looking at Dark Coyote as his head began to spin, and he felt like throwing up. He started to lose his balance - Dark Coyote started his charge.

"Ah, hell, Knife Thrower."

Brackett drew his revolver and pulled the trigger. He collapsed to his knees before knowing if his shot had hit home. He willed himself to stay conscious, and his head cleared enough for him to struggle to his feet and see Dark Coyote on the ground. Dead.

He gathered up Mercy, and the two staggered around the turn where he saw Johnny. Mercy, seeing her mother, ran straight for her and then collapsed over her dead body.

Johnny again raised the rifle, and Brackett put up his hand.

"There is no need to shoot them again. They are dead or dying."

He started toward Mercy. He had gone about twenty feet when he heard the shot and saw Mercy crumple beside her mother. He looked to see Johnny still holding the gun as if prepared to take another shot.

"What the hell is wrong with you? Are you trying to kill your sister?"

"Not no other way," said Johnny, "She be ruinated jist like our mama."

Johnny again pulled the gun to his shoulder and aimed. Brackett drew and fired, and Johnny bounced back with the impact.

He stood for just a moment, looking at Johnny, sprawled awkwardly over the lower branch of a juniper tree. Turning to Mercy, he saw the girl had revived and started pulling herself back to her mother. She cried so her whole body shook. She babbled, but Brackett couldn't understand what she said.

"Are you all right?"

"They killed my whole family. I wish they had killed me, too."

Brackett knelt beside her and saw the slight bleeding where the shot grazed her, knocking her unconscious for a moment. Had Johnny's bullet been half an inch to the right, she would be dead, too. He thought about what she said. She had no way of knowing Johnny had survived the attack at their cabin. She had no way of knowing Johnny had killed her mother and no way of knowing he tried to kill her. He would have to think about how much she needed to know.

Again, he asked, "Are you hurting, Mercy?"

Her vibrating words were hard to understand, broken up with sobs and deep intakes of air, "I have some bruises, and something hit me on the head and knocked me down. Who are you?"

For the first time, she looked up at him, her face covered with dirt, striped with tears flowing like rivers down her cheeks. Brackett took off his outer coat and put it around her shoulders.

"My name is Clay Brackett. I came from Silver City along with your brother, Johnny, to rescue you."

"Johnny! But they killed Johnny with my father and other brother."

"You're right. They did kill Johnny. But not at your cabin. He died just a few minutes ago."

"Just a few minutes ago! How?"

"He was shot while in the struggle to save you and your mother. He is up above."

She turned back to her mother, and the tears started to flow again. Brackett took off his under-coat and covered Minnie's torso with it.

"Thank you." She didn't look at him.

Brackett rounded up a horse for Minnie's body, retrieved his horse and the one Johnny had been riding. Wrapping the two bodies in blankets from the camp, he tied them securely. With a good horse for Mercy, he led them out of the trench. At the top, he stopped to take a last look at its length. Starting the horses toward Silver City, he caught a movement in the distance. On the far side of the flat, immerging from the lava flow funnel, he could see a huge, lone figure walking steadily up the hillside with giant strides.

CHAPTER TWENTY SEVEN

As they rode along, slow but steady, Mercy would go quiet and then erupt into hysteria. Screaming, sobbing, and thrashing. The horses would shy aside. Brackett wished he had something to say. Something to ease her pain, but he knew nothing would be of any use at this time. Time and only time would help settle the girl's feeling of loss and being lost. If he reached across to touch her for reassurance, she would jerk away as if being attacked. Mercy had way too much to absorb. So, he rode beside her in silence.

It would be a long ride to Silver City. He believed Mercy's best chance for healing in Silver would come through the tender touch of Beth. She would know how to help the girl. At least the girl would have someone who cared for her.

"You sure you are not in too much pain, Mercy? We can stop whenever it gets too bad. We have a long ride ahead of us.

One of the few times when Mercy seemed a bit settled, "Oh, I don't care about me, Sheriff. I feel dead inside. What pain I have just lets me know I'm still alive, but I'd rather be dead."

"Uh, how old are you, Mercy?"

"Old enough to be interesting to bad boys, I guess. I turned fourteen last Saturday. Why?

"Just wondering. As sheriff, my job is to treat you as a young lady and make sure we safely get back to town. It will be late tomorrow night when we get there." He hadn't told her he had turned in his badge. He hoped the idea of him being sheriff would somehow comfort her.

"So that means we can't just ride on through the night and get there when we get there, Sheriff?"

He watched her scratch her horse behind its left ear. "I wish I didn't care about nothin' like this horse. Just like this horse don't care about nothin' exceptin' eatin' and drinkin'."

That bit of calm reflection marked one of the few times she seemed relaxed and not ready to explode into another panic.

"I know a little about what you are feeling," he said. "My family was wiped out completely by a renegade gang a few years back. I never got over it, and for a while, I just wanted to get even and later curl up in a ball and die. The only thing that kept me going, I found out other people care if they find you are hurting, and they can offer some kind of comfort. I know folks in Silver City who seem to care about me, and I am not the best company to them sometimes. So, I think they will try to help you. You should let them."

"Sheriff, I didn't know. I saw you pull out that flask a while ago, and then you put it back in your saddlebag. My daddy drank whiskey when he felt bad. Does whiskey help?"

"Hmmm. Good question, Mercy. I used to think so. It drowns your sorrow and takes away most of the hurt for a while, but it all is temporary, and then you are hurting again. It may be costing me the most important person in my life. My advice is do not get started with the stuff. My best time is when I am trying to help someone else, not when I'm drinking."

"Like now, with me?"

"Now? Hmm, well yeah, I guess. You are somebody special, after all."

She rode in quiet contemplation from then until well past sundown. Brackett heard her saying something softly over and over and wondered if it might be a prayer or part of a song. He found a basalt overhang with a spring oozing cold water. The horses began grazing on grass. Brackett took four short lengths of rope from his saddlebag and hobbled the horses after removing the saddles and blankets and laying out the bodies.

He carefully laid the two bodies of Johnny and Minnie twenty feet below another rock outcropping. Mercy watched his every move. He would like to have ridden on through the night, but not with these four horses. The two carrying bodies were easily spooked, and he didn't want to take any chances with them. He didn't sleep much but fed sagebrush to the fire. The girl had his coat and three blankets taken from the band of raiders. They would no longer require them. One saddle had a bedroll tied to it, and he used it's slicker and two blankets for his covering while she used the other bedroll. He built up the fire when dawn began to show.

He offered her food, of which she ate little. It took more than ten hours to finish their journey. They arrived at the stable in Silver City at 7:30 the following evening.

He took the girl, still in deep shock, to Beth. Mercy seemed to feel at ease with Beth right off. Beth shewed him away and after taking the bodies to the undertaker for burial, he spent the night in his room where, for the first time in his memory, he did not drink. It had been many nights of sleeping on the ground and he was exhausted. He still had the nightmares, but slept soundly and awakened to bright sunshine.

When he went into the café the following morning, Beth told him Mercy agreed to stay with her for the near future. The girl insisted on working in the café to earn her keep.

When he went to the jail, Phil Bannon presented him with an unexpected letter from New Mexico. As it turned out, his adopted family in Santa Fe, the Morgans, said Bert Morgan had been offered the position of Territorial Marshal of Southern Idaho Territory. Their letter suggested a strong interest in making the move.

CHAPTER TWENTY EIGHT

It had been more than seven months since Mercy and Brackett made the trip back to Silver City. He had taken Mercy to Beth, not knowing what else to do with the girl. Beth quickly took over, moved the teen in with her, and put the girl to work in the café. They were now inseparable, and Mercy had begun the long healing ordeal.

Bert and Annie Morgan followed the first letter with another letting him know Bert had indeed accepted the position of Idaho Territorial Marshal and would be leaving Santa Fe for Boise in the following May.

Bert Morgan, the man who spent years after the wagon train massacre, trying to find the mother and child. After leaving his mother and Buha, Brackett's Indian father, Bert Morgan, had become a mentor. Bert had been the wagon master when the Indians made their raid back in 1843. He lived only because he had been left for dead. When he eventually regained consciousness, he found all of the people in his charge had been killed. All except for two. The Brackett woman and her year-old son. They were not to be found.

Bert Morgan always believed they had been taken by the raiders and decided he must find them. It took him more than fifteen years, but finally, he found them living among a group of highland Indians, far up in the Owyhee Mountains. These were not the same people who killed the folks on the wagon train. Clay Brackett's mother had married the people's chief, and the couple added more children to the family. While she had no desire to leave, the decision had been made. The boy, then sixteen years old, would go with Morgan to be educated in the white man schools.

The Morgans housed him, fed him, and treated him as one of their own. Bert and Annie Morgan, their son Rand and daughter, the one everybody called Sis, had treated him like family. Rand had gone to college with him and felt more like a brother than a friend.

He knew Bert Morgan had a hard time turning down a new adventure and his wife, Annie? Just like him. Brackett had some fond memories of Santa Fe before leaving to find his Indian family in the Owyhee Mountains, and he wished to see the town one more time. Knowing he most likely would never make the trip if not for the Morgans being there, he figured if ever he was to go, the time had come.

If they were to make a move, it would be sometime in the spring, and he would like to accompany them. Maybe offer a little extra security for their trip. He had no desire to stay in Silver City, and even though late in the year to be making such a journey, he decided to launch into it.

In mid-October, Brackett walked into the Sheriff's office and greeted Phil. After getting scolded for the twentieth time for getting his friend into the position of Sheriff, he finally got Phil to allow him to tell what he had in mind.

"Well, damn, Clay. Can I go with you? Those kids are still raising hell. I'm tired of telling their old men about what they've got into this time. Now they're jumping onto the boot of the stagecoach and riding it into town. Yesterday they landed so hard it broke the strap buckle, and half the luggage fell off."

Brackett chuckled and said, "You know you were made for this job, and I know you love it."

Phil Bannon smiled and nodded.

"Look, Phil, I need a favor. It will be months before Plato is back to being healed. I will come back for him next spring, and I think Jackson will take good care of him but, I would surely appreciate it if you could check on him once in a while."

"You can depend on it. I'll miss ya. Ya'll be careful."

They shook hands, and Brackett went up to the stable to say goodbye to Plato.

Before he left Silver City for Santa Fe, he had one more person with whom he needed to talk.

He found her just closing up for the night. He had suffered through the day with all the demons inflicting him. But that day, he took not a single drop of bourbon or any other liquor. Brackett thought he might die on the spot, but he needed to be completely sober for the conversation he hoped to have.

"Good evening, Beth."

She jumped with the words and turned to face him. "Clay! You liked to scare me to death!" But then she laughed.

"I am sorry about that." He took off his hat and held it with both hands in front of him. "Would you have time to walk with me a bit?"

"Of course. I sent Drew and Mercy on home early. Things were slow."

As they strolled down the street, past the closed shops and the bank, Brackett tried to think how to put what he had to say. The pain in his gut hurt, but he determined he would not let it show. They walked across the creek and up toward the school. They didn't talk, just enjoyed the rare October evening. So warm, she didn't even need the shawl she had on her shoulders.

Finally, as they sat down on the school's steps, Beth opened the conversation. "You're leaving. That's what you came to tell me, isn't it?"

Brackett turned to face her and almost got lost in her eyes. "How did you know?"

She smiled, "Oh Clay, I sometimes think I know you better than you know yourself."

He chuckled and nodded. "I suspect that is true."

He fiddled with his hat before continuing. "The Morgans are going to be moving this way in the spring. I want to help them with that. I also want to spend some time in Santa Fe and the people there before they leave.

If I go now, I'll have the winter there and be able to help them pack everything before the trip."

Beth studied him for a little before saying, "You're hurting. Your stomach hurts, doesn't it?"

"I was hoping you wouldn't notice."

"You haven't been drinking today?"

"I needed to be clear-headed to talk with you this evening."

"You didn't need to be sober to tell me you are leaving." She looked as if she might have a tear in the corner of her eye.

Brackett turned, looking straight at her. "No, I didn't. But I need to be sober to ask you this question. Beth, I know I will either quit drinking and get rid of whatever it is that torments my insides, or I will die in Santa Fe."

She began to object, but he put two fingers to her lips, and she waited.

"Beth, I have never been any good at expressing my feelings. I guess I have never told you how I feel about you, and I am sorry for that. I want to tell you now. I love you, Beth. I have since the first time I really looked at you after getting shot. Back when you brought my meals to me for the better part of my first week here in town."

Now the tear didn't remain in her eye. Joined by more, it slid down her cheek.

Brackett reached over and wiped a couple of them away.

Beth pulled a hanky from her sleeve and dabbed at her eyes. "I guess those are words I've always wanted to hear from you. But I always knew you loved me. I have always loved you, too. I just wish things were different."

Brackett nodded his understanding. "That is what I want to talk to you about. I will be gone until next spring if I can survive. If I come back, I will not be drinking, and I will have beaten whatever this devil is inside me. I just want to ask if you think you might be here for me if I do come back?"

She came near to knocking him over as she lunged to engulf him in her arms. His hat fell behind him, and she held him so tight he thought he might not be able to breathe. Her tears washed down the sides of his cheeks.

At last, she pulled back to look him in the eye. "You go, Clay Brackett, and you come back to me. I'll be right here waiting for you!"

EPILOGUE

Although Brackett took a good supply of bourbon with him when he left Silver City, it lasted only into the third night. He leaned against his saddlebags, having eaten his supper of bacon and biscuits. After sipping on his third cup of whiskey, he found himself again thinking about his last conversation with Beth. Suddenly, he stood up, emptied the cup on the fire, and watched it flare. Then he turned to the saddlebag containing his bourbon, picked it up, and before he could think further, tossed the entire thing into the fire. The flasks broke, and the fire roared, and Brackett grinned.

Unlike previous trips to and from New Mexico, his southwestern trek had been uneventful, but he found exhilaration in once again being alone in the wilderness. He ran into every weather condition one could imagine and found every event to his liking. He slept better than he had for years.

For the first two weeks after burning his bourbon, he suffered greatly. All the symptoms he had been dealing with previously seemed only to intensify. Added to them were the shakes that imitated a man freezing to death. At times he thought he might die, and other times, wished he would. He fell off his horse more than once as everything hit him simultaneously. He twisted his ankle, re-opened one of his shoulder wounds slightly, banged his already aching head, and had to chase down his horse in a snow storm. Most of the time, he would have sold his soul for a single shot of anything with alcohol. Still, when in control, between the horrendous bouts of a recovering alcoholic, he loved every minute of the venture.

His first realization of change came when his head stopped spinning, and the headaches disappeared completely. Gradually, he noticed the stomach pain begin to subside. It still presented itself, but little by little, it grew less and less. By the time he reached Santa Fe, his hands had stopped shaking, and he awoke each morning, looking forward to the day. He knew his hard-drinking days were behind him. Never again would he let bourbon or any other vice rule his life. He began to let himself think about a life with Beth. Even about that little cabin with the two kids playing by the stream.

Once in Santa Fe, he spent hours with all of the Morgans, but mainly with Rand at his law office. Often, Rand would hang a closed sign on his office door, and they would spend hours exploring the surrounding area. Far from town, they relived their college days, practicing their fast draws. Brackett couldn't hide his surprise at how fast Rand still drew and fired. Certainly quicker and more accurate than anyone else he had ever run across.

"You have continued to practice, have you not?"

"Oh, maybe once or twice since I last saw you," Rand smiled.

They laughed and felt a brotherhood they had both missed. They talked about their past adventures, and Rand admitted he held no excitement about the amount or type of business he got in Santa Fe. He wanted some adventure.

Bert Morgan accepted the position of Marshal of Southwest Idaho Territory. Rand's mother, Annie, sold her hotel and stood ready to follow Bert wherever and whenever he wanted to go. As they talked about the pros and cons of the Marshal job, both grew excited about the new prospects. When the date was set for heading to Boise for the job, Rand, after serious thought and no small amount of encouragement from Brackett, decided to make the move with them.

The winter passed slowly, and Brackett began to feel restless. Similar feelings among the Morgans grew day by day. By spring, Bert Morgan had made all necessary preparations and set a date in Boise to take over the Marshal position. Rand closed his law office, and the family purchased two schooners for the trip to Idaho Territory.

The only sadness interrupting the excitement came with the idea of leaving behind Sis and Alex Freed. Sis, the youngest of the Morgans, loved the ranch life and her new husband. The young couple was committed to Alex's family, and leaving the place never occurred to anyone. Ranching: the only life Alex had ever known and the only life Sis had ever wanted.

There were lots of family suppers that spring and long evenings spent talking and reading, and planning. Tears were not uncommon within the Morgan get-togethers as the day of departure drew ever nearer. Promises were made about travel to and from, but everyone knew they might never see one another again. Perhaps if travel someday became safer, perhaps then.

On the first day of May, the long and dangerous trip to Brackett's mountains began. Two other families joined in the adventure, following Bert Morgan's lead. Four wagons, pulled by four head of mules each, left the town of Santa Fe. Bert was strict on what each wagon could contain, knowing what lay ahead. Before leaving, the other two families, at first disgruntled but eventually understanding, sold their heirloom furniture and took only more minor, lightweight belongings. The little train of adventurers was into the wilderness by noon, and Bert rode back to the first wagon, driven by Annie and flanked by Brackett and Rand.

"Well, boys," Bert said to Brackett and Rand, "We've made this trip before. Who wants to scout ahead first?"

Brackett looked at Rand and grinned. Rand nodded back, winked, and they both spurred out ahead at a dead run.

About the Author

Neil James is a lifelong resident of Southwestern Idaho. His heritage goes back to the very first days of Silver City. His great grandfather arrived in June of 1863 just weeks after the Discovery Group found the first gold. He did well as a miner and later as a business owner. He owned portions of several mines. One of his sons, the author's grandfather, partnered with him in business. Neil James father was born and raised in Silver City and later lived and worked on the family's cattle ranch. So, Neil's interest in the area and its history is strong. His stories, while fictional, are based on an accumulation of characters and stories passed down through family since the 1860's. As a youngster, his family spent every possible weekend in the Owyhee high country. As he got older, he ventured off on his own, riding horses and motorcycles in the mountains that stand guard over the Snake River Plane far below. His love of the mountains has never wavered. He spends much of every year roaming the canyons and high deserts that he writes about. His hours in the back rooms of the Owyhee Historical Museum researching old newspapers and stories of the area keep his understanding of those pioneers always in the forefront of his mind. He revels in the chance to tell their stories, albeit with some fictional license.

He lives below the Owyhee Mountains near the Snake River, where he is at work on his next novel.

You can contact Neil via email at:
Neil.james.writer@gmail.com
He'll look forward to hearing from you.

If you enjoyed reading BRACKETT, check Amazon for the next chapter of the Brackett/Morgan series. If you would like to be notified when it is available and/or be added to Neil's mailing list, just send a note to:

Neil.james.writer@gmail.com

Made in the USA
Middletown, DE
28 July 2024